EMAILS OF THE DEAD

EDITED BY
ANTHONY GIANGREGORIO

OTHER LIVING DEAD PRESS BOOKS

TWISTED FISH: AN AQUATIC ANTHOLOGY
PLANET OF THE DEAD
GHOSTLY TALES OF TERROR
HALLOWEEN TALES OF TERROR
THE JUNKYARD
THE HAUNTED THEATRE
THE DEAD OF SPACE BOOK 1 AND 2
PLAYING GOD: A ZOMBIE NOVEL
ZOMBIES IN OUR HOMETOWN
DROPPING FEAR
HERE COMES SANTA
UNITED STATES OF ARMAGEDDON
STORIES FROM THE WASTELAND
THE TURNING: A STORY OF THE LIVING DEAD
JUST BEFORE NIGHT: A ZOMBIE ANTHOLOGY
THE BOOK OF HORROR * KNIGHT SYNDROME
THE WAR AGAINST THEM: A ZOMBIE NOVEL
CHILDREN OF THE VOID * DARK DREAMS
BLOOD RAGE & DEAD RAGE (BOOK 1& 2 OF THE RAGE VIRUS SERIES)
DEAD MOURNING: A ZOMBIE HORROR STORY
BOOK OF THE DEAD: A ZOMBIE ANTHOLOGY VOLUME 1-5
LOVE IS DEAD: A ZOMBIE ANTHOLOGY
ETERNAL NIGHT: A VAMPIRE ANTHOLOGY
END OF DAYS: AN APOCALYPTIC ANTHOLOGY VOLUME 1-4
DEAD HOUSE: A ZOMBIE GHOST STORY
THE ZOMBIE IN THE BASEMENT (FOR ALL AGES)
THE LAZARUS CULTURE: A ZOMBIE NOVEL
DEAD WORLDS: UNDEAD STORIES VOLUMES 1-7
FAMILY OF THE DEAD * REVOLUTION OF THE DEAD
RANDY AND WALTER: PORTRAIT OF TWO KILLERS
KINGDOM OF THE DEAD * DEAD HISTORY
THE MONSTER UNDER THE BED * DEAD THINGS
DEAD TALES: SHORT STORIES TO DIE FOR
ROAD KILL: A ZOMBIE TALE * DEADFREEZE * DEADFALL
SOUL EATER * THE DARK * RISE OF THE DEAD
DEAD END: A ZOMBIE NOVEL * VISIONS OF THE DEAD
THE CHRONICLES OF JACK PRIMUS
INSIDE THE PERIMETER: SCAVENGERS OF THE DEAD

THE DEADWATER SERIES

DEADWATER * DEADWATER: Expanded Edition
DEADRAIN * DEADCITY * DEADWAVE * DEAD HARVEST
DEAD UNION * DEAD VALLEY * DEAD TOWN * DEAD GRAVE
DEAD SALVATION

COMING SOON

BOOK OF CANNIBALS VOLUME 2
DEAD ARMY (Deadwater series book 10)
CHRISTMAS IS DEAD VOLUME 2
DEAD HISTORY 2
MONSTER PARTY

EMAILS
OF
THE DEAD

EDITED BY
ANTHONY GIANGREGORIO

EMAILS OF THE DEAD: A ZOMBIE ANTHOLOGY

Copyright © 2010 by Living Dead Press
ISBN   Softcover   ISBN 13: 978-1-935458-82-1
                     ISBN 10: 1-935458-82-5
All stories contained in this book have been published with permission from the authors.

All rights reserved. No part of this book may be reproduced or transmitted in any form or by any means, electronic or mechanical, including photocopying, recording, or by any information storage and retrieval system, without permission in writing from the copyright owner.

This is a work of fiction. Names, characters, places and incidents either are the product of the author's imagination or are used fictitiously, and any resemblance to any actual persons, living or dead, events, or locales is entirely coincidental. This book was printed in the United States of America.

For more info on obtaining additional copies of this book, contact:
www.livingdeadpress.com

FOREWORD

Collected in this book, are the lost emails found in the basement of a large internet provider. The server was all but destroyed, but some of the data was recovered.

When the data was sifted through, more than two thousand emails were found, most too corrupted to read. These are a few that were recovered fully intact.

It's believed these emails never made it to their destination, and that friends, family, and loved ones never found out what the last thoughts of the senders were.

And that is what this book is for. To give voice to those lost souls, so at least someone will have read these emails, and in doing so, for one brief moment, bring that person back to life.

For though now gone from this earth, as long as our dead remain alive in our memories and in our hearts, they are not truly dead.

Date: 17 July 2010 16:53
From: Buddy <basballfan44@gmail.com>
To: Tom <tommyjones67@fastmail.com>
CC: Michael D. Griffiths
Subject: Before the lights go out

Hey Tom,

I'm not sure if you'll be getting this. I'm surprised the internet is even still working, but I guess it makes sense that it would be the last thing to go. I wish my cell still worked, but it's long gone. Probably not too many people have electricity anymore. I'm hoping you might still have a way to read this, maybe things aren't that bad yet in Kentucky. I just hope you're okay.

The only reason I even have electricity is because I made it back to the psych ward. They let all the clients go, of course, and the place is shut down, but being in charge of security has its perks, which include... having keys to the building. I'm surprised more people didn't think about coming back here. We have loads of food, secure doors, and obviously the backup generator.

I have it on right now. It's weird to see lights working, even stranger to be on a computer. This is certainly something I would never have thought I'd be doing again. Even weirder to be on this old computer I used day after day at work. I guess after smashing heads open with an axe and seeing my wife get eaten alive, I never thought I'd be doing something like this that used to be so normal.

Remember when we were kids? We used to play end of the world games, but in those games we were always there together, backing each other up. Hell, we had our friends, too. Now though, I have nobody. I wish more people would show up here. I would think that someone else would realize there's a lot of food here, but maybe they're all gone already. Now all this food will just make me live longer.

Sorry, man.

Despite everything, I still want to live, even if it's alone. Over time, I suppose water will be the bigger problem, at least before the food runs out.

I can hear some banging.

Oh damn, maybe these lights weren't such a good idea, or I should have shut them off before I started the generator. A horde of zombies is growing outside. I could have been able to escape before, but for better or worse, I'm trapped here now. I might be able to kill some, because our psych unit courtyard is fenced in. In principle, I'd like to kill as many as I can. It might not matter, but maybe it will. Maybe some other survivors around here will have less to fight one day when it counts the most.

Right, who am I kidding? This sucks. Will you ever even read this email?

This whole situation is like living in Hell. I used to think the world sucked before, what a laugh. We really are in Hell now. Remember how we used to joke about how the zombie plague would be cool? Well, it isn't fucking cool! Nothing could be worse than this. Except going through this alone. That's the worst.

Maybe you'll write back. I hope so, but then again, who am I kidding?

Even if you do, what would it matter? I can't make it five blocks, let alone across five states.

I just hope you're okay. Even if you don't get this, I know you could still be out there, somewhere and be okay. But damn, you got those little kids. That won't make things easy and you're in Lexington. The big cities, I hear they're the worst.

Damn.

I'm just going to hope you're hanging in there. I'm sure lots of people are. That's why I'm not going to give up. I'm going to kill as many of these bastards as I can. I'm serious. Bring 'em on. I'll kill some every day if I have to.

Wow, it's getting pretty loud out there. These are tough steel doors though. I'm sure they'll hold. They had better hold…

The front doors are glass. I'm a little worried about those. Still, I can lock that part of the building off. I'll still have the food and some medicine. Hell, I'll even have beds. As long as it rains enough, I'll be able to last a while.

I can probably escape if I need to. I'm just not sure where I'd go, unless I heard from you. Which brings up the next point, the generator fuel is only designed to last seventy-two hours. Of course, I won't be running it all the time, but even if I conserve it, the internet could always go out. If I hear from you, I'll head out there, or maybe you could come here. Who knows?

Wait, I'm hearing something. I better go make sure things are cool. Or at least lock the inner doors. I'll try to write again. Write me back as quick as you can.

I have to go.

Love

Your big bro

Date: 16 July 2010 11:54
From: Tina <TinaWilliams@medent.com>
To: David <DavidRhyer@hotmail.com>
CC: Terry Alexander
Subject: Mike's at the door

Davey

Where are you? I tried calling your cell, but you won't pick up. I know the lines are down including cell service. I only hope you check the emails on your Blackberry.

Mike's at the door. He arrived just after I got home from work. I came inside and kicked my shoes off and there he was, beating on the front door. Thank God it's solid. He's circling the house now, moving in that awkward gait of his. I can see him every time he passes the window. I don't know why he showed up; he's never been this far from the South Canadian Border before.

He looks awful; the hot months have really taken their toll on him. His lips and ears are gone, and part of his nose is missing. His skins all dry and leathery and it's stretched as tight as a drum across his bones. He's a walking skeleton. Good thing he's slow, at least I can out run him. I'm going to get the shotgun; I wish I'd have paid more attention when you showed me how to load it.

Wish me luck,
Tina

```
Date: 16 July 2010 12:13
From: Tina <Tina_Williams@yahoo.com>
To: David <DavidWilliams88@hotmail.com>
CC: Terry Alexander
Subject: Mike's at the door
```

I couldn't load the shotgun, so I got your pistol instead. It's next to the keyboard as I type this email. I hope you get here soon, that constant circling is starting to worry me. I wish he'd go back to the river and eat some dead fish or something.

I hear barking. I guess Emily Summerfield's dog, Dolly, is still loose. I know I was griping about that dog, now I'm glad its here. Mike stopped outside the den's large window, and he gave me a bird's-eye view of the action. That dog was really raising hell with Mike. He was trying hard to catch that feisty pooch. She kept nipping at his legs then dancing out of reach. It was almost funny. Her ears were laid back, hackles up, and she was showing a lot of teeth. That Cocker Spaniel sure has some moxie.

Then they moved away from the window, but I can still hear the barking. Maybe Emily and Joe will come after her, and drive Mike away. A few minutes ago I saw someone coming through the hedge, and it was Emily. Oh My God! She was one of them; Mike must have gotten to her. As I watched her, there was a line of drool running down her chin and she' had dried blood around her mouth. Dolly just kept yipping, and now she's whining. I'm going to check the other windows and see what's going on.

```
Date: 16 July 2010 12:20
From: Tina <TinaWilliams@medent.com>
To: David <DavidRhyer@hotmail.com>
CC: Terry Alexander
Subject: Mike's at the door
```

Joe's here, too. He and Mike caught Dolly. I don't know how they did it. She was howling and whining and trying to get away, but Mike had a good grip on the poor dog's hind legs. He bit her. He sank those grimy choppers into her shoulder. I watched him spit out a hunk of bloody hair and take another bite. Dolly's blood squished through his teeth and dripped down his chin. My God it was awful. Then Joe and Emily got a piece, too, they just tore that dog to shreds. Now I know where they were for the last two days. I think Mike saw me while I stood at the window. I screamed like a school girl and ran back to the den. He circled around the house again, while carrying Dolly in his arms. Joe and Emily were following along behind him like children; this is just so weird. When you get here you're going to show me how to load the shotgun again. I promise I'll pay attention this time.
Mike's getting closer to the house; his decayed face is pressing against the windows as I type this. I dropped down behind the desk in the hopes he'd leave. I know they're looking for me now, the three of them.

```
Date: 16 July 2010 12:27
From: Tina <TinaWilliams@medent.com>
To: David <DavidRhyer@hotmail.com>
CC: Terry Alexander
Subject: Mike's at the door
```

Mike started banging on the outside walls a minute ago. He's searching for a way in; it's only a matter of time before he breaks a window. The other two just began to join in, too.

Where are you? You should have been home half an hour ago. Them circling was bad enough, but I can't stand the banging. Every thump sends shivers racing up my spine. When I peeked out I saw Emily standing at the window; she was just staring at me, drooling like a starving hound.

Davey, I'm scared. I know Mike was a friend of yours before the 'change.' But you should have put a bullet between his eyes long ago. If you had, I wouldn't be in this fix now.

A window just shattered in the living room, I'll be right back.


```
Date: 16 July 2010 12:35
From: Tina <TinaWilliams@medent.com>
To: David <DavidRhyer@hotmail.com>
CC: Terry Alexander
Subject: Mike's at the door
```


Mike broke the picture window in the living room. He was crawling inside when I got there. I tried to keep him out. I shot him three times, but I couldn't hit his head. I snatched up the heavy brass lamp and smashed it across his skull. It didn't even slow him down. I ran back to the den and locked the door.

I can hear him shuffling around in there. I didn't see Joe; I don't know where he is. Mike's like a bull in a china closet, knocking things down and breaking everything.

He just found the door and is now beating on it with his fist. It's not nearly as strong as the outside entry. It's vibrating in the frame and some of the upper panels are cracking. It won't last much longer. I know he's going to get inside. I have three bullets left. Maybe I can get lucky and put one in his brain. If I do I'll make a run for it, I'm sure I can outdistance Joe and Emily.

```
Date: 16 July 2010 12:41
From: Tina <TinaWilliams@medent.com>
To: David <DavidRhyer@hotmail.com>
CC: Terry Alexander
Subject: Mike's at the door
```

Mike just knocked a basketball-size hole in the upper panel. His worm eaten head is framed by the opening and he's leering at me. It looks like Dolly's blood has dried on his face. He looks like an obscene clown. I used the last three bullets to put holes in his throat and jaw, but I couldn't hit his head. My hands were shaking too badly.
Emily's still at the window, so I'm going to make a run for the back door. Hopefully, I'll make it outside. If they kill me, you know what you have to do.

         I love you,
            Tina

Date: 2 July 2010 23:10
From: Nathan <stud812@gmail.com>
To: Jake <prowlingrooster@yahoo.com>
CC: Nelia Thompson
Subject: Wild night

Jake,
You're not gonna believe the night I'm having! We're at that new club, Sizzle. You know, the one that has all the hot chicks dancing around like strippers? Yeah, I finally got in! It's awesome! You can't walk two feet without some drunk chick grinding on you.
Matt is here with me. Don't be mad, I did text you and let you know, but you never got back to me. Your loss. You should see him right now! He's in the middle of a group of chicks, in a dance orgy! Yes, it's that intense! I wish you could have made it. You'd love it here.

There's this super hot redhead that keeps sitting in my lap. She's taking me back to her place when she gets back from the bathroom. How awesome is that? You know how I love redheads! It's gonna be one wild night. She's coming so I gotta go. I'll finish this up and send it to you at the end of it all. I know how you hate having so many small emails. LOL

Just some advice, never let a drunk chick drive. I was scared for my life the entire time. But all the adrenaline really gets me in the mood, if you know what I mean!
She's in the bathroom again. Apparently some jerk bit her in the club. She didn't think much about it at the time, but she said it was starting to burn. Doesn't look like much, just barely broke the skin, she should be fine.
I hear her coming. I don't want her to catch me emailing with my phone, you know how women are. Wouldn't want her to freak, get freaky, but not freak out. :)

Okay, she's asleep. She was amazing! Apparently she does a lot of Yoga, because she was very flexible. One thing was weird in a not cool way, though. Before she fell asleep, she said she didn't feel so well. I think she might have a fever. Damn, I hope she doesn't have the flu or something. That would suck. I don't know that I could miss work for being sick; you know how my attendance is. My boss might go through the roof.
She seems to be sleeping okay. Maybe I'll wake her up. I'm a devil, I know.

Holy shit! You aren't gonna believe the shit that's going on! Remember the chick I was talking about? Duh! You're reading this, so you have to. She fucking died! I tried to wake her up and get lucky again, but she wasn't breathing! I didn't know what to do! I tried CPR, and that didn't work. I was panicking and pacing around the room. I mean, she was dead! What was I supposed to think or do? Then the bitch sat up. Yes, that's what I said! She went from dead one second, and sitting up in bed the next. I thought maybe I'd just thought she was dead, and she was really still alive, but I don't think so, I checked really good.

Then I saw her eyes. They were messed up! I've never seen eyes like that. She grunted and got off the bed. I asked her if she was okay, if she wanted me to call an ambulance, and if she had taken any kind of drugs or anything tonight. She didn't answer, just staggered and stumbled toward me like some zombie-looking freak.

I reached out to steady her, because she looked like she was going to fall down. She wrapped her arm around me, buried her face in my neck, and bit me!

At that point I no longer cared how she was doing. I pushed the bitch off me and grabbed as many of my clothes as I could find. That's why I'm walking down the street without a shirt right now. Plus, I only found one shoe. I probably look like a homeless person.

I got a cab and made it home. I really don't feel good. I think the bitch gave me whatever she had. She was pretty good in bed, but not so damn good she was worth all this shit. I'm burning up and can't leave the bathroom. Every time I try, I start vomiting again. I'm going to go 'head and send this to you. Could you come over and check on me when you get this? Or at least call? I don't feel like calling anyone else, or trying to explain to anyone else what's going on right now, and since I have this email ready to go, you're the lucky one who gets to baby sit me.

I threw up again. I'm hot all over, shaking, and I can't keep my eyes open so I'm done writing.

Don't forget about me, I don't want to be late for work.

Nathan

<Sent from my Blackberry>

```
Date: 11 July 2010 15:51
From: Pete <BigTex@cleds.com>
To: Rachel <RFoxy@cleds.com>
CC: Adam Francis Smith
Subject: Hyperlink
```

Rachel,
Tried to get you on chat, but the room is lagging so bad. There's tons of people on, all trying to figure out what to do. I can't believe this, you're only a mile away but I can't get to you. There's too many of those *things* outside. I want you to know that whatever happens, I love you. I wish I could be there with you, but I know if I leave here they'll get me. I'm hoping the army gets here or something, maybe there's still time to save us. But if not... I know you love me, too, and that's enough for me right now. I can remember every time we ever kissed. Every touch. When I think of those zombies touching you I just want to scream! Don't let them get you, Rachel. If they get in, kill yourself or something. That's what I'm going to do.
I love you.
Pete

```
Date: 11 July 2010 16:10
From: Rachel <RFoxy@cleds.com>
To: Pete <BigTex@cleds.com>
CC: Adam Francis Smith
Subject: Hyperlink
```

Pete! I heard on the radio the army is coming, but they blew up Roerson Bridge by accident and now they'll have to go around or wait for the engineers to get here and fix it.

I know you're scared, but you have to hang on, Pete. You have to be there for me when this is all over. My mom and dad got killed just this morning. They got in the car and Dad just drove right through the garage door and out into the street. They left me, Pete! They just panicked and took off and Dad drove right into the front porch of Bob Zeffers' house across the street, and the zombies got them and pulled them right out of the car, and ripped them to pieces right there. Then Mr. Zeffers came out shooting that big gun of his, but he only had two shots and a zombie pulled the gun out of his hands. Another one grabbed his arm and pulled so hard it ripped right out of the socket! The blood splattered all over the windshield of the car and then Bob went down and half a dozen of those things were on him in a second! I swear they were looking at my house, but then they went off down the street. I don't know when they'll be back. I was so scared. And now my mom and dad are dead.

So you see. I have nobody now. No one but you, Pete. Please hang on. Stay safe. I have to go board up the kitchen door now—the one that leads to the garage. I'm going to move the refrigerator in front of it after I nail it up.

I love you too, Pete. Please be strong.

Rachel

```
Date: 11 July 2010 16:20
From: Pete <BigTex@cleds.com>
To: Rachel <RFoxy@cleds.com>
CC: Adam Francis Smith
Subject: Hyperlink
```

Rachel: OMG! I'm so sorry about your folks. I really liked your dad, and I know your mother loved me and I her.

Because of you, I decided that if they get in, I'll fight, and I will escape. Be sure you find some weapons in case they get in, and make sure you have a way out. I did that. I can get out an upstairs window that faces the street and drop down onto the garage. Knowing you're still out there helps a lot. I have a long steel pipe

I'm going to use to bash their heads in. I blocked all the windows and doors except in the kitchen. That way I know where they're gonna come in from. I'll be ready. If it weren't for you, I would have given up already. I would have just opened up my front door and walked out into the street and let the bastards have me. But I want to see you again, Rachel. I want this nightmare to be over so we can start living our dream. I want to marry you and be a father to your babies.

I saw some of them down at the end of the block. I have just my bedroom window open now and I can see down the street. You know that shirt that Jack Preddy used to always wear, with that little kid pissing on the flag? Well, one of them was wearing that shirt. I think it was Jack. He's a zombie now. I tried to see if it was him for sure by using my binoculars. All I could tell was that the hair was sort of the same, but his face was all crusty with dried blood and one of his eyes was hanging out of the socket, bouncing off his cheek as he turned his head. His earring was gone, too, the skull head one from his left ear. Well, the whole ear was kind of gone. The shirt was covered with blood and ripped up a lot, but I could still tell it was Jack's. I don't want to become a zombie, Rachel. I don't want them to get you either.

I've made up my mind. I'm going to risk it. I'm coming to you. Stay where you are. I'll use the signal, okay? So you know it's me when I knock. Then you can let me in and we can fight together, or escape, or die together. Whatever, as long as we're together. I love you Rachel. I'm on my way!


```
Date: 11 July 2010 16:30
From: Rachel <RFoxy@cleds.com>
To: Pete <BigTex@cleds.com>
CC: Adam Francis Smith
Subject: Hyperlink
```


Pete! You're crazy! Don't come here! There's too many of them. One of them was climbing up the side of the house, but I was able to knock the trellis away with a broom stick and it fell down onto the grass. It got up again, but it went around the house. I can hear pounding in the kitchen and at the front door. I can see more of them coming down the street! Don't come here, Pete! I'll come to you. I'll sneak down the gutter or something and come to your house. The zombies are coming from the other direction, so it shouldn't be too hard.

Just stay where you are! I've got a gun. I took it from the drawer next to my parents' bed. It's loaded and I know how to use it. Just stay put, and when I get there we can figure out what to do next. I'll use the signal when I get there so you know it's me. Just wait for my knock. I'm coming now. I love you!

Date: 11 July 2010 16:42
From: Pete <BigTex@cleds.com>
To: Rachel <RFoxy@cleds.com>
CC: Adam Francis Smith
Subject: Hyperlink

Rachel! I just saw your last email to me. I didn't get it. I was already out on the street and couldn't check my email. You aren't here! I put the trellis up and climbed into your room. I had to kill like seven zombies with my steel pipe, just so I could get a clear path to the side of your house. There are at least a hundred on your block. I don't know how you'll get past them. I told you to wait for me! I'm covered in all kinds of zombie shit. Oh God, it stinks so bad. I guess you're on your way to my house. I hope you make it. I'm going to go back home. I hope you're there. I love you so much!

Date: 11 July 2010 16:48
From: Pete <BigTex@cleds.com>
To: Rachel <RFoxy@cleds.com>
CC: Adam Francis Smith
Subject: Where are you?

You're not here! Rachel! Where are you? I'm hurt real bad, Rachel. I killed so many zombies I lost count. They're everywhere. I saw John Maples get torn apart and his wife shot herself in the head right in the parking lot of the grocery store. I took the gun. I'm already out of ammo. Where are you, Rachel?

I had to fight my way back to the house. I couldn't find a way in until I dragged a bird bath over from next door and used it to climb back up onto the garage. I'm not going to be able to hold them off for long. I've got my pipe, but I'm tired. I'm bleeding, too. One of them bit my shoulder and tore a hunk of meat right off. I shot it in the face and then bashed its head in. I think it was Mr. Jefferson. I think most of these zombies are people we used to know.

Where are you, Rachel?

There's so many outside now, they followed me!


```
Date: 11 July 2010 17:03
From: Pete <BigTex@cleds.com>
To: Rachel <RFoxy@cleds.com>
CC: Adam Francis Smith
Subject: I love you
```

Rachel?
    I love you. They're in.

Date: July 2010 13:14
From: Will <Willtrent@hotmail.com>
To: Tim <Tim7theman@juno.com>
CC: Anthony Giangregorio
Subject: Dinner Party

Hey Tim,

What's up?

Listen, I don't think I'll be able to make it to your dinner party tonight. I'm afraid something's come up, something beyond my control.

See, I'm trapped in my car and there are zombies swarming the highway.

There's at least ten of them banging on my car right now and I don't know how long the windows will be able to handle their pounding.

The zombies are something else, all covered in rotting flesh and pus. They're ruining the paint job on my car. Hell, I just got it washed yesterday. Why is it always like that? You wash your car, spend the ten bucks, and bam, a zombie outbreak arrives.

So anyway, I had heard from Greg in accounting that Cheryl was going to be at your dinner party. I heard she was hot, and man, I wanted to meet her. But I guess you'll just have to say hi for me in my place.

I would have called but I left my cell phone at the office and luckily I had my laptop with me in the car.

Man, they are really pounding on the windows, slobbering over the glass. They remind me of Pavlov's dogs and I guess I'm the dinner bell.

Funny, whenever I thought about how I was gonna die; it was never as the Blue Plate Special for a horde of zombies.

But, hey, win some, lose some, I guess.

Oh, wow, looks like the guy in the car next to me just lost a bet. He actually opened his door and tried to make a run for it. He didn't get far. He made it like ten feet before he was brought down by an old bag with half her face missing. Oh sweet Jesus, they're tearing into him like he was a cooked chicken at a homeless Christmas dinner. He's screaming something fierce but there's no one to help him. Not me, anyway. I'll stay here in my car till either the traffic moves again or the zombies get to me.

So anyway, about Cheryl. I hear she's easy, is that really true, Tim? I can't say I'd want to marry a woman like that but I would sure have some fun with her for a while. I'd treat her like a car I'd leased once. I'd ride her hard, put a shitload of miles on her, never change her oil, then trade her in for a new model. Ha, am I a cold SOB or what?

Oh, shit, they just got another traveler, a woman in her midtwenties. She was in a Volvo but its safety features didn't seem to save her from an assload of zombies. They broke her rear window and then crawled into the car as she screamed and cried out for help. There are so many bodies in the car I can't even see her anymore.

LOL, it's fucking hilarious the way they're all in that one car; like clowns at the circus.

Yeah, I know, Tim, you're thinking I'm taking this all in stride, that I don't seem to be too afraid of dying in the most agonizing way possible—by being fed on. Well, you know what? That's horseshit man. I'm fucking terrified, but hell, crying about it isn't gonna change it. Either I'm gonna live or I'm gonna die, I can't change it, so why bother?

Oh crap, a zombie picked up a brick from the side of the road and is coming right for me. Damn it, the dead bastard is using it as a bludgeon to break my driver's side window! Here he goes, he's using it! What the fuck, I thought zombies were supposed to be stupid?

Now there's small marks on the surface where the corner of the brick connected with the glass the first time he hit it, and he's pulling his arm back again!

This time is gonna do it, and it looks like I'm gonna have to wrap up this email.

So listen, Tim, it's been great knowing you and if there's enough left of me to reanimate, I'll still try to get to that dinner party. Hell, maybe I'll take that bite out of Cheryl yet! LOL, a little zombie humor for you.

Oh, shit, the window just shattered and the zombies are reaching in for me.

Well, I'm gonna sign off, Ow, fuck, one just bit my shoulder. And more are climbing into the car as I type this.

Fuck, get off me you damn pusbag! Shit, sorry, Tim, I didn't know I was typing still, as I am in searing pain as they feast on me flesh. Oh, Christ, one just ripped into my stomach and blood is shooting everywhere. I can't see the damn screen anymore.

Well, this is me, signing off, saying see you in the afterlife, or whatever the hell is waiting for us............

```
Date: 25 July 2010 07:56
From: Kristyne <KristyneB56@bellsouth.net>
To: Jason <JasonQMiller@hotmail.com>
CC: Brianna Stoddard
Subject: Good riddance to you!
```

Hello Jason!
Didn't think you'd hear from me again, did you? Well, I was saving your email just for this. Since this will probably be our last time talking before we're both dead, or walking cannibalistic corpses. I need to tell you exactly what I've had on my mind these

past few years. Hooray! Time to shut up and listen to *me* for a change!

Okay, first of all what did I see in your lyin' cheatin' ass? What kind of mind fuck did you put me in, seriously? What I saw was an emotionally attractive person who loved kids. But what I should have seen was Satan's ugly little helper. So I get pregnant and think for a while the baby is yours. We move far away from my hometown and you choose the big city you grew up in. You helped me with everything and you acted like a sweet fairy tale prince. I fell so hard for your ingenious act. Little did I know you were planting the seeds of destruction in my life from that very first time frame. How was I so stupid not to see the danger?

Well, only about a month or two after moving into our 'perfect' apartment together, you started getting jealous and abusive and controlling. Then I was stuck far from home without a friend in the world. I stayed caged up in the apartment like an animal while you worked and partied and slept over at God knows whose house.

Why couldn't I just run away then? Well, because like the bastard you are, you made sure I had no family and no friends to come to my rescue. I should have known you were nothing but a no good asshole! Oh, and another thing as well, you thought you could make me mistrust myself… Yeah right. I know what I saw and felt in that awful place was real, and what *you* were doing was the *only* problem. You pushed me down when I was pregnant and called me names. What the hell made you want to do that?

Then as the baby was ready to be born you turned into a charming prince again. I shouldn't have expected it to last very long. Only two or three weeks after my son was born, you decided to be rotten to me again. Well screw you for that! I tried to avoid you when humanly possible and even started to pray you would go away to fuck someone else so that you'd be too busy to hurt me. Of course my wish was granted and I had more time to be with the baby and myself to appreciate not getting teased or mentally tortured. But the more you scoured the earth for new pussy, I began to feel lonely and left out. So I went out to find some attention and much-needed romance of my own. And the more you hurt me and abused me, the more I wanted to blatantly throw it in your face. I would have given anything to see you crushed from watching me kiss another man and hold him tight!

The first time you abused my child, I finally had enough. That's why I left you and got the law on my side to protect me and my baby. I really thought that was the end of it all. Wow was I wrong! I got stuck in a vicious custody battle with you for almost a year and a half. I fought the whole situation and got you to get a paternity test. THANK GOD MY SON WASN'T YOURS! I was shaking and crying from so much joy when I read those words on the test results!

Things finally looked hopeful after being lost in despair for so long. But I still had to fight and struggle out of the situation because I had to prove just how bad the situation was for us. Well, it was definitely a rough road to take, but in the end I won because the judge saw the truth. No amount of sucking up and lying witnesses on your side could blind the judge from the truth. HA! I won my freedom you jerk! Good riddance!

So I went straight home to my family and have been better ever since. I've had the chance to make a better life for myself and my child. I don't know whether or not I could say the same for you. But I really don't care.

Now we come to the most exciting part of this email.

You've deserved my hate and my scorn and now you deserve this awful fate spreading across the world. May your eyes that once feasted upon others be ripped out of your head. May your black heart be chewed up like a hamburger and your hands that caressed others and inflicted pain on me be torn apart or crushed with excruciating pain. May the walking dead stomp upon your genitals while they carve you up like a large steak. I'm wishing you the best, most agonizingly painful death that they have in store for you. I'll go to sleep better knowing that you will be next on their menu… Good riddance, Kristyne

```
Date: 2 July 2010 15:48
From: Mark <markcrenshaw55@live.com>
To: Jim <Jimmycooper2008@yahoo.com>
CC: David Renfrow
Subject: Business 101
```

Hey Jim,

I think I'm going to be late for that meeting with the clients from Asia. I'm stuck out on I-95, in bumper to bumper traffic. I don't know what the hell is going on. You been listening to the news today? They're saying that the dead are coming back to life. I tried to call in, to let you know that I'm stuck out here, but the phones are down so I am sending this email from my Blackberry.

…Oh sorry, I got distracted. I think that they're right. The dead really are coming back to life. A bunch of them are attacking a Greyhound bus about a quarter of a mile in front of me. I'm jammed in here pretty bad, but at least they won't be able to get me. I have the windows rolled up tight, and all the doors locked.

So forget the clients, if the dead really are coming back to life, there has to be a way we can make money off of this. Remember, it's all about diversifying our options. We should invest in a gun manufacturer or ammo supplier; we'll make a boatload of cash. Have the guys and girls down in R&D start working on a 'zombie repellant.' I don't care if it's made out of Earl Gray tea, if we can't sell it here in the states, we'll just ship it to one of those Third World countries overseas.

As I'm sitting here and watching, some of these damn things are moving closer to my car. A bunch of them are women, and being dead is not doing anything for their appearance. Maybe we should develop some type of cosmetics for 'today's zombie woman on the go.'
'Course, we probably won't be able to sell it until the government gets a handle on all this.
I gotta go. I'll get to the office when I can, but it might be a while. Two of these damn zombies just broke out the rear window of my Benz.

ffffffffffff
One of them bit me!
ggggffhh

Date: 22 July 2010 15:14
From: John <JPEvens@DPowersMutual.com>
To: Mark <Mark5@Descartes.com>
CC: Chris Deal
Subject: Be careful!

Mark,
Buddy, if you get this email, I need you to do something for me. Lock the doors, get the gun from the safe, load it like I showed you, don't take the safety off until it's time, and take your mom and your little brother down to the basement.
I can't believe I'm asking you to do this. Things aren't right out on the streets. People are going crazy. When I left for work this morning, I thought it'd be a regular day, you know? I'd be sitting at my

desk, wishing I was at home with you all. We'd go out for ice cream and take in a movie.

Things were fine until I got into the city. I thought I'd a start before the traffic would begin, but it was bottlenecking at the exit for I-85. Once I was past, I saw what was going on: four cars smashed to rubble on the side of the road. One thing about Charlotte, the drivers here can never resist gazing at someone else's misery. You've heard me rant about it before, I know. It can be a damned fender bender or a flat tire and every person out there will slow down to get an eyeful.

Thing is, and I know you're not going to believe me, but the thing is, some of the people in those cars were still alive, still moving around.

And they were eating each other.

A man was down on his back on the side of the road, and a woman was on top of him, her teeth deep in his throat. She ripped it right open. Another woman, wearing what used to be a nice pantsuit, was stumbling towards the cars passing by. Her left leg was broken, the bone sticking out just under her knee, but she kept shuffling forward, trying to get at the cars as they passed. There was a big gash down the middle of her face, the blood coming out black and thick. She gnashed her teeth at me as I drove past her, not five feet away.

I should have turned around right there, I know. I'm sorry I didn't. I thought, it could be anything, dope heads or maybe I took my sleeping pill too late last night, maybe I was dreaming—one of my coworkers, he had a bad reaction to that stuff. He got up one morning, dressed and got into his car, drove past his exit, rear-ended someone, and just drove back to the office. He came in and placed his head down on his desk. A minute later he jumped up, not knowing how he got there.

I pulled off the interstate at my exit, and things were weirder there—cops shooting people, people eating people.

I hope to God I'm dreaming this, I thought.

There were less cars there than normal in the parking lot. It was like I was sleepwalking, just going through the same motions I do everyday, not quite seeing what it was I was seeing. When I got out of my car, there was this shuffling and Bill, my manager, he was just standing there.

I don't know what happened, but that wasn't really him. He had a bloody hole in his neck, the same black stuff pouring out all over his $200 shirt and his suitcase open in his hand, a trail of papers leading back to his car. The blood vessels in his eyes must have burst, they were completely dark, empty, but he saw me. He started towards me and, well, I ran. Not back to my car, of course, that would have been the smart thing to do. Never was all that smart, after all.

I booked it to the entrance to the building. The door was open, thank God. I didn't think to lock it, though.

Remember when I brought you into work a couple years ago? My business is on the top floor, four stories up. I pressed the button to call the elevator down. It was up top and was slow as always. When it dinged to indicate it was on the third floor, Bill started hitting the front door. It was nothing but glass and started to crack with his second impact. The elevator was still at the second floor when the entire pain of glass fell out of the door and he stumbled in, his hands reaching for me.

Around the corner is a corridor that leads to another office suite and the stairs. I ran for it just as the elevator door opened and Marsha, the secretary for my company, spilled out, her white satin blouse completely covered in blood, her eyes dark, a low moan slipping from her lips.

There weren't any on the stairs, thank God. The door for our suite was locked and I kept knocking and yelling until Jimmy opened the door and pulled me in.

He was the only one who'd made it in, out of forty employees, it was just the two of us. Not sure if you met Jimmy when you came in. He's all right, I guess. Most days I'd say he's pretty boring, but today he's my best friend.

Neither of us had any clue what was going on. I tried calling you guys at home but the phones weren't working. My cell won't go through either.

I don't know what to do, bud. We can watch TV here in the break room and it looks like it's the same thing going on all over the city.

No clue if it's just here in Charlotte or all over the country. I sure hope not.

I don't know if I can make it home. Please, I know you check your email all the time. I've given you crap for it before, and I'm sorry. Please, get my gun and take your mom and brother down to the basement. Make sure the doors are locked and move the china cabinet to block the front door. Take a radio down with you, too. And please be safe. I don't know if those things are up in Huntersville. If not, do what I tell you. If the police come by to evacuate the area, go with them. If the police are still around, that is. I'd hope they call in the Guard, but there's no telling if that'll help. I think this thing may spread too fast for them to be effective.

Jimmy and I were talking just now. We've got all the doors secure, I don't think those things can get through. Hell, here's hoping they can't figure out how to open the doors. Up top we've got a complete view of the office park. There aren't too many of them out there. I can see a lot of them on the streets. There are a few cops firing on them, but it seems like every time they take one down, two more take its place. It looks like if you shoot them in the head, they go down for good. If you have to use my gun, remember that.

Jimmy wants to stay here, keep an eye on the news, but if it clears up, he's going to head home. If I can make sure the roads are clear, I'm coming home, too.

Bill's still out there. He went back outside, and he's just circling the parking lot. He still has that suitcase swinging open. Christ, least I don't have to deal with him anymore. He was always a pain in the butt.

Damn it, I have to try. I can't stay here waiting. I'm going to run for my car. I'll try I-77. This time of day it's usually clear. Hopefully everyone who fled went south. If I can get north, it should be a straight shot. I'm coming, son. If I can get back, I will. And I'll never miss another one of your soccer games again. I love you, bud. Tell your mom and brother I love them, too. I'll be there as soon as I can.

Love,
Dad

```
Date: 16 July 2010 17:19
From: Cindy < Cindy_newton@hotmail.com>
To: Chelsea <ChelseaMalone@yahoo.com>
CC: Brianna Stoddard
Subject: I need you to get over here!
```

Chelsea,
Holy shit! What the fuck is going on out there? This is totally f'ed up! I went out to meet my mom at work after school and everyone there was like rotting and shit. It looked like Night of the Living Dead. It was totally messed up. I puked all the way home from seeing people ripped apart and eaten and blood squirting everywhere. OMG! What the hell could have done this? I think my mom turned into one of those things. What am I supposed to do, Chelsea? What do you think we should do if more of those things start attacking everybody? Would you at least let me know if you're all right and if you can try to make it over here? I'm counting on you because I know you're much smarter than I am and you might know what to do. I really hope you can make it! I'm so scared now and I'm running around like a headless chicken, trying to block all the doors and windows. You'll have to let me know if you're coming so I can try to watch for you before I block the front door. I think the chain lock might be strong enough to hold them back for now. I don't think they can break through it. But I'll block it off when you get here, all right?
I wish your parents would have let you come over after school like you should have. They NEVER let you do anything! Grrr! Now I have to worry about you crossing town to get here safely. I'd hate

to put you in danger, but I need my best friend here with me right now and I really want to be able to get through this with you. So please get over here or let me know what you're doing ASAP. Bring your family with you if you can. They're welcome here, too. Shit! I hope no one else is dead and I hope whatever this is isn't spreading. Someone out there might be able to fight it or fix it, assuming they can find out what it is before everyone ends up the same or dead. Goddamn it! I hope it never comes to that! WTF am I supposed to do if I'm the only one left alive? I CAN'T HANDLE THIS KIND OF PRESSURE! I WAS SUPPOSED TO GET MY FREAKIN' NAILS DONE TONIGHT FOR PROM!
What the hell can I do now? I better calm down before I hyperventilate… OMG! Something broke in!
OMG!
OMG!
OMG!
OMG!
 We're all gonna die…
We're all gonna die…
We're all gonna fuckin' die!

mbkjlstv?tkzdqxztw

xxxxxxxxxxxxxxxxxxxxxx

```
Date: 21 July 2010 12:56
From: Billy <wild_billy@lpm.com>
To: Martin&Sheila <hendrixfamily@comt.net>
CC: Rebecca Besser
Subject: Trapped at school
```

Dear Mom and Dad,

We've just been informed by our teacher that we can't go home, because of the zombie outbreak. They don't know where the zombies came from, but there are hundreds of them around the school. It's a good thing they have all the doors locked, to keep people out, otherwise we probably would have been overrun before lunch.

They've assured us there's enough food for everyone and they've told us all to email our parents, as the phones are down, but the net is still up. Maybe you'll even send me an email back before the power goes out. I don't know if it will, but according to all the zombie movies, it'll happen sooner or later. Do you think everything that happens in the movies is true? Like if you shoot them in the head, they'll die? That's what I'm going to do, if I should have to try and kill one. Not shoot them, but hit them with something, right in the head.

Despite everything, and the reassurance of the teachers, I'm scared. I know we don't have enough food for all of us, for a long period of time. Eventually, we'll either die of starvation, or we'll have to leave.

Most of the kids are crying. I'm scared, too, but I'm not going to cry. It won't help anything. I'll still be stuck here, waiting to die.

Dad, I'm sorry I yelled at you last night. Well, I'm sorry I ever yelled at you. I know you love me, and just wanted to protect me and make me happy. But I needed you to give me some space and didn't know how else to communicate that to you. I wish I would have gone to the races with you, like you asked me to, instead of insisting on going to the mall with my friends. I'm sorry I didn't help you around the house more. I remember how much fun it was working on things with you when I was younger. I don't know why I was so stubborn.

I love you, Dad. If I live through this, I hope I'm just like you when I grow up. I hope that I can be a good dad, too, just like you. You've really done a wonderful job. I just wanted you to know that.

Mom, I'm sorry I didn't clean my room more often. I'm sorry I didn't put my dirty laundry in the hamper like I should have. I know I made more work for you, when you were already tired from doing so much to take care of me and Dad. I'm sorry for all the times I yelled at you for not making the food I wanted to eat, or not doing something just the way I wanted. I know you always worked hard to try and make me happy.

I wish I wouldn't have stopped hugging you. I know it broke your heart when I started pushing you away, insisting I was too big to be hugged. I would give anything to feel your arms around me right now, and to have the smell of your hair surround me. To feel you rub and pat my back. I love you more than I can ever say. Thanks for everything.

Oh shit, I can hear screams. They found a way into the building. The halls are a blood bath. The teacher is trying to hold the door shut, but she isn't strong enough. A couple of the guys from the football team are trying to help her.

Damn, one of them just got bit, and the teacher and the other player have been pulled out into the hall. They're screaming.

There's nowhere to go. I'm going to keep on typing until I die. I want to make sure that the last moments of my life are spent with you. I love you both so much.

Zombies are swarming into the room, falling on each person they come across. I'm in the back corner of the classroom, kneeling on the floor so they can't see me as I use the keyboard on my lap. Blood is everywhere. It's shooting from a girl's jugular, spraying the ceiling. The zombies are feasting and basking in the spurting blood. They look like they're having a buffet.

Oh no, one has spotted me. He's shambling over, and almost upon me.

Did I tell you I love you? Well, I do!

His hands are so cold. His mouth is descending toward me. This is it, I'm gonna die!

Oh God, it hurts, he's eating me alive. There is so much blood I can't see the letters on the keyboard; they're covered in red.

I can't…keep…my…eyes…open…

I love you,

     Billyyyyyyyyyyyyy………………..

```
Date: 15 July 2010 13:58
From: Brad <BradMM56@hotmail.com>
To: The Watkins <Watkinsfamily@medent.com>
CC: Mariah Deitrick
Subject: Justice for Julia
```

Dear Mr. and Mrs. Watkins,

I know I'm the last person you wanted to ever hear from again, but I'm hoping what I'm about to tell you will give you some relief and justice for Julia.

I'm not trying to ask for your forgiveness, or wash away my sins. Instead, I thought the details of my death would help you find piece in your final hours.

Before I'm gone, I do want to assure you that I loved her. She was my wife after all, but I shouldn't have been driving so fast on that gravel road. I take full responsibility, and now I get to pay for what I did. You both said you wanted to see me behind bars, but I guarantee you that this is going to be far worse.

Soon, the living dead will barge though my front door and find me. There's nowhere to hide, and I'm out of ammo. I'm going to become zombie kibble. I only hope they kill me, and not turn me into one of them like they did my neighbor.

I watched as they sunk their teeth into his flesh over and over, blood spraying everywhere.

When I thought he was dead, the things walked away, and he slowly got to his feet. It was like he was unharmed.

I don't want to get back up like he did!

Oh geez, it's starting! I can hear glass shattering downstairs. I guess I should have tried to board up the windows and doors! Pushing furniture in front obviously didn't help.

I'm not going to lie and say I'm not scared, because I'm scared out of my mind right now! I'm shaking so violently it's difficult to type this email to you, but I have to. I have to keep going until the end. Hitting 'send' will be the last thing I do.

Okay, I just looked out the window. There's a whole flock of those creatures moving toward my house. There's no sign of life—well *real* life. I must be the only one left in my neighborhood, and that's why their drawn to me.

Shit! Now, I'm really scared! I can hear sounds of fighting from downstairs. They must be fighting over me. Oh wait! They settled their fight. I'm facing the reflection of the winning man behind me in my computer screen.

I can't bring myself to turn around. Instead, I'll keep typing. That seems more sensible. There's nothing I can do about him, but I can help you in your final hours by giving you a play-by-play of what's happening to me.

Consider it as justice for Julia!

Damn, those things are fast. It took a chunk of flesh off of my back, and I didn't even see it coming. It was almost as though the zombie didn't move, but the pain I'm in proves it did.

I can feel the blood running down my back. It's pooling on the seat of my chair. It feels like I peed my pants, but it's only blood—for now!

Crap! There goes another piece of me. This time it was the back of my head right above my neck. I should hit send now, but I can't. I can't bring myself to end this final email. It's the last thing I will do in this life. Wow, I never thought sending an email to you would be my finial act, but I didn't intend on being eating by zombies either.

There's more of them now. They're attacking from all sides now. I have one chewing on my leg, another on the side of my head and eating my ear, and one more on my shoulder.

It's getting harder and harder to type. I can feel my body shutting down, and it's a good thing I don't need to see to type this because I have blood in my eyes. I can't even move my hands off the keys to wipe them. My only hope now is to try and end this and find the 'send key' before its too late.

I hope this email finds its way to you! I need you to know I've paid for killing Julia in that car accident.

Tell her sorry for me when you see her!

Brad

```
Date: 13 July 2010 16:57
From: Jennifer <Jennifer_Jones@hotmail.com>
To:<dentistjohnny@live.com,beeman2374@inlook.com,
candyman73@zmail.com,birdladyc6@hotmail.com,
c2gu_barbara1968@gmail.com,chipman@earthlink.net,
Dalebrotter69@yahoo.com, Budlit@hotmail.com>
CC: Brian J. Smith
Subject: Goodbye all!
```

To whomever,

If you're reading this, that means I didn't make it. Of course I didn't make it or else I wouldn't be writing this email. But dead or alive, someone needs to know what happened. I won't bore you with some stupid scene break, cut into the past and then pull you back into the present like most people do. If my wife Natalie had still been alive, then she'd be the one writing this and not me. Sad part was, she'd gone out to check the gas gauge in the Taurus when they surrounded her and tore her apart like a Charleston Chew; a shotgun with eight shells can't hold back an army of twelve.

Besides, I told her to stay in here, told her we were fine right where we were but she doesn't listen. Claustrophobia, cabin fever killed my wife—not the walking dead. No, I didn't stutter. The walking dead; as in horror movies; get the picture?

No one knows why the dead are walking, and in the end, I guess it doesn't matter too much. All that does is that they're hungry and are attacking everyone they can get their hands on.

Natalie perished last week. The bars on the windows and the two shotguns that *were* posted at the front and back doors were only enough to give you that sense of power a gun loves to give. I would've saved Natalie, maybe even traded places with her, but the shotgun was too far away and there were too many of them. It's not that I didn't want to do it. The only shotgun available was out of reach and if I'd gotten it in time, they would've already bit her so the idea in itself was useless. I would just have had to kill her myself later on, anyway.

The booby traps I set up a week ago have been used up and my ammo is depleted. Eight shells left in my shotgun which, in case we forgot, isn't worth dick in the face of an army.

I feel guilty about Natalie. I would've done anything to have her back right now, anything. It's not my fault she doesn't listen to me. She does whatever she wants to do no matter what I say. You can only say so much before you give up and let them learn on their own.

Right now, the four zombies at my kitchen window glared at me like a zoo exhibit, baring blackened gums and yellow teeth. The four dead cheerleaders at my back door would've been perfect *Playboy* cover girls if they weren't dragging their intestines with them. From the look of the bars on the windows, the next good breeze would blow them away.

The boat still has some gas in it; maybe I could create a diversion and speed away from this little shithole. The beach is three blocks away, a gray blue body of water that pounded the rocks at night and swayed gently under the moon. A perfect escape...if I can reach it.

A few minutes ago, the front door caved in and hit the floor so hard it rattled the windows. Two adults, another dead cheerleader and a ten-year old boy stumbled into the house, baring coal-cannibal grins wet with hunger. They shoved me to the floor and the cheerleader straddled me while the other three gnawed at my stomach and legs.

I managed to kick them off and get away and now I'm in the closet with my laptop, the screen the only light. But I'm bleeding really bad and well, we both know what happens when you get bit.

Oh well, at least I won't have to worry about doing my makeup and my hair anymore.

Sincerely,

Jennifer

```
Date: 20 July 2010 09:27
From: Joyce <cherry_pop@smail.com>
To: April <kismet60@line.com>
CC: Rebecca Besser
Subject: I'm sorry
```

Dear April,

I don't know if you'll even read this. You'll probably just delete it, if you don't have me blocked. I know you hate me, but I still think about our friendship. I mean, it lasted for years and years. We've spent our whole lives together. Remember when we were ten, and we ate popcorn and drank grape soda till we puked? Or that time I had a slumber party for my thirteenth birthday, and we decided to try beer, daring each other to sneak a couple of bottles out of the fridge? Damn, we were really messed up, weren't we? Our parents were so pissed!

I know it's pathetic, but I miss all that stuff.

I'm really sorry I kissed Jake. I knew you liked him, but I did it anyway. He was so cute, and I had a crush on him, too. But now I see how stupid it was to throw our relationship away on a boy. I hope you can forgive me.

The zombie outbreak seems to be getting worse. My dad said it would be taken care of, and the government was trying to scare us, so they could control us. He was wrong.

None of us have left the house for almost two months. The fuel in the generator is almost gone. I'm just glad we have cable internet, it seems to be the only thing still working—for now. But even so, it's sketchy.

We ran out of food yesterday and my dad left this morning to see if he could find us more. It's now dark. I don't think he'll be coming home. There are just too many zombies out there. He's probably dead. He's probably one of *them* now.

Holy shit! I heard the front door bang open, I have to go see what's going on.

I'm back for a second, but I don't know how long. They're in the house! The zombies; they're coming! They're having trouble getting up the stairs, but they'll make it eventually. I don't know what to do. I can't escape through the window, there's a horde of them outside.

I locked my bedroom door and pulled the dresser in front of it. I hope my barricade holds. I don't want to die! Not like this! I don't have any weapons either. I guess I could use my laptop and hit them with it.

I wish you were still my friend. I wish I could have talked to you about all this. You always understood me. I've been lonely without you. This year at school has been terrible. I saw you in the halls and wanted to talk to you, but when I tried, you ignored me. You know, I actually entered the bathroom and locked myself in a stall to cry whenever that happened. I've had detention uber times this year because I was late for class.

They're at the door! I'm so scared, my hands are shaking. I want to throw up and cry at the same time.

Oh, God, they've broken the door. I see a bloody, festering arm reaching through. I can smell them, and see their rotting faces through the broken wood.

Just so you know, Jake was an ass. He cheated on me with three other girls! Can you believe that? In actuality, I saved you from the heartbreak of loving that jerk. I know it doesn't make things better, but I just wanted you to know.

The door's open and they're in my room. I don't want to die, but there's no way I can fight them all off. Oh, God, my mom is one of them! My mom wants to eat me and kill me! How messed up is that?

They're trying to drag me away, from my computer, from you. But I need you to understand, before I die, that I love you like a sister. I just hope you're still alive to read this!

Oh God, some dead guy just bit off my toe, and I'm bleeding. The others are still trying to figure out how to get at me in this corner.

Blood is shooting out of my foot and covering the floor. They keep slipping and falling, but the toe biter is still holding my foot, lapping at my blood like a dog drinking from a water hose.

I'm feeling weak and dazed...

I'll never be able to tell you how sorry I am that I hurt you.

Everything's going dark…

I love you. Your BFF forever,

Joyce

```
Date: 8 July 2010 12:20
From: Eugene <Zombiephreak88@hotmail.com>
To: Mom <Sweetums543@yahoo.com>
CC: Anthony Giangregorio
Subject: I miss you Mom
```

Dear Mom,

I'm getting worried as you haven't returned home from the store yet and I know you didn't bring your cell phone. I saw your lap top was missing from upstairs so I decided to email you.

I'm scared, Mom, I don't like being alone. I know I'm twenty-one and I should be more mature but I can't help it. And of course it doesn't help that my acne is so bad the kids in the neighborhood call me Pizza Face and that I've never been able to get a girlfriend. I know that you know I'm a virgin because I told you a few months ago when we sat up late and had one of our 'special talks'. And even if I met a girl, once I tell her I live in my parents' basement, she'll pretty much lose interest.

The zombies are still outside which makes me worried for your safety.

They can't get in the house, though, I'm safe.

The internet is still up and I'm keeping busy on it. I just got through leaving this really mean and scathing review for this writer I found on the internet. I found some stuff that anonymous people said about him and though I have no idea what's true or made up, I believe it anyway as we both know my IQ was never the highest.

Yes, Mom, I know, you would call me a sheep, someone who believes anything I read on the internet. But isn't that the truth? After all, if it wasn't true, it wouldn't be posted there.

But as I am writing this, I might as well be honest. Truthfully, I have no idea what the writer I left the review for is like. For all I know, he's the nicest guy in the world, or the biggest asshole. See, I'm too scared to email him personally, so I troll the internet and say mean things about him.

Yes, I know what you'd tell me, Mom, but what can I say? I'm a petty man and have no life.

As I look out the basement windows and see the zombies out there, I know I'm gonna die a virgin. My dick has only known the sweet touch of my right hand, and that on one too many occasions.

Maybe it's your fault, Mom. Maybe if you had raised me better and Dad hadn't left us one night. Maybe if you had taught me right from wrong and how to treat other people with respect. I blame the internet, the cesspool of corruption where every asshole gets his say, no matter whether it's relevant or not.

'Open mic night', someone said of the internet; say what you want, say the first thing to come to your mind, but don't worry about how factual it is. If it's in print, then it must be true.

I can't help but think about that writer I slandered and harassed, though. See, he wrote zombie books and now look what's happening outside? I wonder if he's doing well, after all, you write enough about zombies, doesn't that mean you can survive an outbreak of the walking dead?

Maybe I should have befriended the guy instead of attacking him for no good reason. For all I know, he lives on the next block, and if he had been my friend, he could have helped me.

Oh, well, water under the bridge.

So, Mom, when are you getting home? My underwear needs to be washed and I need you to cook me dinner.

Pathetic? Me? Yeah, I guess so, but hey, what do you want from me? I mean, I spend my free time harassing people on the internet. But I have to admit, as I'm such a loser, at least if they talk to me I can somehow feed off their fame and get attention for being an ass. It's better than being ignored, I suppose.

Oh shit, I heard a crash from upstairs. I'm gonna go check it out and I'll be right back to finish this email.

Oh, Christ, Mom, they got into the house! I ran down here, and I know I shouldn't be typing anymore, but I need to finish this. I have a feeling this might be the end for me.

When those zombies broke in, they really looked at me like I was an actual pizza. I ran from them but as you know I'm overweight and I couldn't move that fast. I heaved my bulk through the doorway as the man boobs on my chest bounced like Bo Derek's perfect breasts in the movie 10.

You remember that movie, Mom? I do, I jerk off to it all the time. I do a lot of that as I have never had a woman. Oh sorry, I already said that. You'll have to forgive me, but I have to say it's a touchy point with me.

Oh God, they're coming down the stairs! There's no place for me to hide in here either. As you know, it's just my bed, bureau, desk with my computer—my only way of feeling like I'm part of the world—and the washer and dryer. I thought about hiding in the dryer but it seemed pointless as I'm way too fat.

Oh Jesus, there's Janey from next door! She's sixteen and oh so hot. Remember that time she caught me jerking off to her in the bushes as she sunbathed in her backyard? That was embarrassing. Actually, she doesn't look that bad right now. Her throat is torn out and the blood has coated her shirt. But that's good news 'cause now I can see her nipples pressing up against the material. And they look so perfect.

There are three other zombies with her and I need to take care of them.

BRB.

Okay, I'm exhausted, but I killed the three zombies that were with Janey. I used my old baseball bat—the one I never used for playing the actual game—and I cracked their skulls open.

Janey I didn't kill, after all, she may be dead, but she's still looking good. And best of all, if she's technically dead, then she's not underage anymore.

So to sign off Mom, be safe out there in the zombie world and do me a favor if you do make it home?

Knock once on the basement door before entering, because in a few moment's I'm gonna be busy.

I guess I won't die a virgin after all.

You know what? Maybe this whole 'the dead walking thing' will be good for my social life; after all, I'm not that picky.

Your son,

Eugene

```
Date: 10 July 2010 10:24
From: Holly Sanders <hsanders@99mail.com>
To: Richard Jones <richardj@richardson2010.com>
CC: Hollister Ann Grant
Subject: They're here!
```

Richard,
The zombies are in Gettysburg, too. They're not in our subdivision yet, but Barbara said she saw them on Route 30 by the Giant Food. She said one of them was so rotten his arm and big chunks of his face fell off. After a car ran over him, he peeled up his carcass and staggered into Walmart.
The radio said a busload of Kansas tourists went to the Evergreen Cemetery to see the spot where Lincoln gave the Gettysburg Address.
The zombies were lurking around the graves along the tree line where nobody noticed them until it was too late.
Bill thinks they'll move on to Biglerville by the end of the week.
We're going to wait them out here in the attic. He brought up all the canned food and the Diet Coke.
I'm just worried about Sparkle. You know how poodles love to bark. I'm scared to death she'll bark if they come in the yard and give us away.
You know, Richard, you've been such a wonderful brother over the years. We're all going to pull out of this, but just in case, I want you to know you're the best brother in the world.
                    Love,
                    Holly

```
Date: 10 July 2010 11:28
From: Richard Jones <richardj@richardson2010.com>
To: Holly Sanders <hsanders@99mail.com>
CC: Hollister Ann Grant
Subject: They're here!
```

Holly,

I saw one of them thirty minutes ago in the bushes of the house across the street.

He wasn't walking like a normal guy. A dead giveaway—pardon the sick pun, but I haven't slept in two days.

When he turned around, his eyeball was hanging down on his cheek and his nose was just a black hole with a worm wriggling out like old spaghetti. His head was lolling around and some clumps of meat fell out. Then he cracked a window and smashed his way inside the house.

Nobody's in that house, BTW. The Millers made a run for it this morning. They threw everything in the Volvo, clothes, golf clubs, flat screen TV, and took off for South Carolina. I just hope they made it out of town. I was laughing at them, but I should have jumped in the back seat.

Oh crap, oh crap. I see three more. Good God, they're making this horrible moaning sound.

OH NO, THEY HAVE MRS. WILSON. WHY DID SHE COME OUTSIDE TO FEED HER CATS, WHY, WHY? OH NO, THEY BIT HER LEG. She hit them with a bag of cat food. Oh, my God! They gnawed off her arm! I can't believe it!

I've got to hide in the basement. You and Bill are the greatest and will always have a place in my heart.

Your loving brother,
Richard

```
Date: 10 July 2010 12:22
From: Holly Sanders <hsanders@99mail.com>
To: Richard Jones <richardj@richardson2010.com>
CC: Hollister Ann Grant
Subject: They're here!
```

Dear Richard,

Bad news. Ten minutes ago somebody broke a window downstairs. It's been quiet since then, but we think one of them is in the house.

Sparkle almost barked, but I held her tight and looked in those big brown eyes and said, "Mommy says no, don't you bark, Sparkle," and I KNOW she understood me.

Oh, no, I hear heavy footsteps. Heavy, like a Frankenstein moving around. I hear two of them. Some zombies are coming down the hall, making these awful sounds, "Runch, runch, runch." What does that mean, 'runch'? LUNCH?

I hope Sparkle doesn't bark! I've got to go.

Love you,
Holly

```
Date: 10 July 2010 13:29
From: Richard Jones <richardj@richardson2010.com>
To: Holly Sanders <hsanders@99mail.com>
CC: Hollister Ann Grant
Subject: They're here!
```

Dear Holly,

Bad news here, too, because the zombies are outside my house. I'm holed up in the basement with my trusty shotgun, and if they try anything, I'll blow their faces into sushi. Man, I never thought this would happen.

I can see their feet going by the basement windows. Wormy curled-up skin with the toes flaking off. Oh, my God, there went a whole foot!

The basement door is rattling! They keep moaning!
Love you forever,
Richard

```
Date: 10 July 2010 13:35
From: Holly Sanders <hsanders@99mail.com>
To: Richard Jones <richardj@richardson2010.com>
CC: Hollister Ann Grant
Subject: They're here!
```

Dear Richard,
OMG, they're downstairs in the hall closet, and I don't think they see the pull-down attic stairs. Bill's ready to fight them.
We're watching them through a crack in the floor. Oh, they're horrible. Their heads are so rotten their brains are falling out on my brand new white carpet, and they have this awful smell of decomposing flesh, and they keep moaning.
I'm trying to keep Sparkle from barking. I have my hand over her snout. Bill says to throw her out the window, but I'd never do that, not in a million years. I'd throw him out first.
Richard, if you're still there, write me back, please.
Your loving sister,
Holly

```
Date: 10 July 2010 13:42
From: Richard Jones <richardj@richardson2010.com>
To: Holly Sanders <hsanders@99mail.com>
CC: Hollister Ann Grant
Subject: They're here!
```

FIVE OF 'EM! THERE'S FIVE OF THEM! THEY'RE COMING IN, THEY'RE COMING IN! I'm gonna go Rambo on 'em!
Richard

```
Date: 10 July 2010 13:45
From: Holly Sanders <hsanders@99mail.com>
To: Richard Jones <richardj@richardson2010.com>
CC: Hollister Ann Grant
Subject: They're here!
```

Richard, are you all right? Are you all right!

```
Date: 10 July 2010 13:57
From: Holly Sanders <hsanders@99mail.com>
To: Richard Jones <richardj@richardson2010.com>
CC: Hollister Ann Grant
Subject: They're here!
```

Richard, are you still there? You haven't returned my last email,
Richard? Email me back, please.
Oh no, Sparkle just barked.

```
Date: 17 Jul 2010 20:51
From: Paul <PaulFRobbinson@medent.com>
To: Marisa <Dental_Assis63@comcast.net>
CC: Domenic Giangregorio
Subject: Goodbye
```

Dear Marisa,

This may be my last time to talk to you so I'm going to make it my best. I'm hiding in the attic with my laptop. Zombies were trying to get up the ladder.

I'm sorry. I'm so sorry about everything. It's just that, it's all falling apart here and I can't believe what's happening. A zombie made it up to the fifth step. I took my shotgun, loaded it and shot the zombie. A zombie's severed hand grabbed hold of my ankle. I tried to knock it off with the butt of my shotgun and it finally came off with a few whacks. I ran back to my laptop just to write again.

One of them almost got up but I stopped it, thank God. I heard a loud moaning come from outside the attic window, but when I went to check there was nothing in sight.

Now where was I? Oh yeah. I think it's best to just forget about me and live your life to the fullest. I'm not going to be alive for much longer. Earlier, when the windows shattered, I covered my face with my arms to deflect any glass. Hands were hanging on and zombies were climbing up the side of the house. To conserve ammo, I kicked their hands. Their fingers broke off and it was enough to knock them down.

I'm just getting off track now.

What I really wanted to talk about was my feelings for you. The way you smile. How even if someone were to do the worst thing in the world to you, you wouldn't yell or hurt them. You would just talk to them and settle things in a calm manner. But the best thing about you is your eyes, in my opinion, the way they sparkle off of shiny objects and when someone looks into your eyes, they feel like they're on top of the world. Shit, a couple of them made it up the steps. Right now I'm writing with one hand and shooting with the other. I'm trying to reload with one hand and still keep on typing at the same time. Dammit, a head and torso crawled up to my leg and took a big chunk out of it. I think he got bone,

too. There's a lot of blood coming out. I'm getting woozy. I can barely even see straight.
One of them is trying to reach for my neck. If you're somewhere, anywhere and still alive, all I want you to know is that I…love……

```
Date: 17 July 2010 16:14
From: Wayne <modernwfre@live.com>
To: Billy <halo2rocks56@comcast.com>
CC: Gary Lucas
Subject: What's up?
```

Yo dude,
Well, it's finally happened! After all my preparations for this day, and I get caught at the office with only a stapler as a means to defend myself. At least that bitch Janice from accounting got it before me. She's with the rest of them moaning at my door. You should see her hair; you'd piss your pants. She's got blood all down the front of her fake Armani and her arm has a bone poking through, it's hilarious. Anyway, I thought I'd get an email out while the power's still on. I've been taking in the news from around the world about the zombie outbreak, it's crazy. You would think the army would have coped better, but to see the world go to shit as quickly as it did is nuts. I really wished this would have happened on a Saturday, then I could have just gone to my bunker and had some fun with my Uzi.

I'll just sit it out here for a bit, getting the latest from CNN and play some COD-4 online. Join me in some fragging if you can, you camper bitch.

Here's my sit rep. I have six hungry zombies at my door including that jerk Greg, that Homo Stan and that bitch Janice plus three others I don't know, that are possibly from sales. I have the door barricaded and I can't reach the water cooler. My weapons check is a stapler as I already mentioned, some pens, and a hole puncher. I thought maybe I could use the waste paper bin as a helmet if I poke some eyeholes in it, but I'm still deciding on that as I already took a piss in it and I must be dehydrated or some shit because it smells bad. Looking around, I also have a pedestal fan I can use to hold them back with or as some kind of battering ram.

Right, that's my plan then, COD-4 until the power runs out then its piss smelling waste paper bin on head, pen in one hand for eye stabbing, fan in the other for ramming, then I make a break for my bunker. I should look pretty funny but it's a plan. Join me at the bunker (Mum's basement) if you can. I have the generator so we can fire up the Xbox and my stash of sweet herb. MMmmmmmm.

Adios Amigo, keep it real.

PS. I tried my Jedi mind powers on these assholes..... it didn't work.

```
Date: 18 July 2010 11:26
From: Keith <keithmerter66@bellsouth.net>
To: Margaret <MargieWalton@gmail.com>
CC: Brianna Stoddard
Subject: Saying goodbye
```

Dear Margaret,

Who knew the end of the world would come so swiftly? We all thought this summer would be so pleasant and promising, but now look at us.

But I didn't write just simply to talk about that. I needed to tell you how much you mean to me and how much I feel sorry for the time we've lost. If I would have known what was going to happen, I never would have spent so much time at work and took you for granted. Now we're on separate ends of the Earth, you in Paris while I'm in Thailand. I can't even see your face one last time before we're either eaten alive or turned into horrid monsters ourselves. I try to push out the images of your mutilated body feeding hundreds of pale white zombies.

I can't imagine how your good looks would be greatly demolished by the effects of becoming infected. If you ask me, I'd call it Hell. I'd choose cancer any day compared to what will happen! Shit, just hearing about the symptoms on the news that if you're bit, you're pretty much dead, is painful enough to hear.

First, you get so sick you wish you *were* dead, becoming delusional. They say it's like a really bad flu. It's like you're either shitting or puking out your whole internal body.

If the pain and fright of that doesn't kill you, then you live on as a mindless cannibalistic eating machine when you return from dying. At least by then you wouldn't give a fuck whether or not you ate your best friend and you wouldn't feel any more pain. Neither of those fates is pleasant. I wish we didn't have to go through this at all, but there's nothing we can do about it now. We're all doomed to become one of those monsters or get eaten by them. It's not going to be escapable forever.

I hope you've at least been able to read this email before your demise. I wish you the best of luck, even though that doesn't seem to help now. I pray there is still a miracle out there waiting to happen. If not, we can all guess correctly that humanity will be permanently extinct. Hey, at least we had a shot at living this long. Maybe if our mistakes would have been corrected long ago this never would have happened. But it's all water under the bridge now. We shouldn't be angry over what couldn't have been predicted. Enough of the what-if's and the should-have-beens. I need to go out like an honorable man. I need to face death without regret. I'm going to load my gun and wait to pull that trigger. If they discover my hiding spot, I'll go quickly instead of waiting for them to finish me off. I want you to know I'll always love you. And I hope you get to choose the same way out as well. That is a better fate for you. I hope to see you on the other side soon!

Your faithful and loving husband,
Keith

```
Date: 18 July 2010 14:29
From: Dale <Dale_walker@yahoo.com>
To: John <John_manners@hotmail.com>
CC: Jeff Kelly
Subject: Hey!
```

Hey John,
Just checking in from down here in sunny Texas. Not much new to report down here, other than the usual. You know, just hanging out, trying to exercise when I can, watching a movie now and then and fighting off the occasional band of walking corpses. Man, does my life sound dull or what?
Sorry, you know that sarcasm is the weapon of choice when combating the blues associated with that pesky apocalypse. Actually, does this qualify as the apocalypse? It's certainly got several characteristics of what I'd consider one. It's somewhat apocalyptic,

right? I guess I never understood if the world was supposed to actually end during an apocalypse, or what. Too many episodes of Buffy, I guess, since it seemed like they were dealing with an apocalypse every other week. Just sort of 'Ho hum, off to algebra and then time to stop the world from ending, just another boring day in Sunnydale.'

Man, sorry to rant. It's been so long since I've actually spoken to anyone that I just can't seem to stop myself. All of this random conversation has just been dying to escape, and now that I've actually learned someone else is out there, it's flowing pretty darn freely. Lucky you!

How are you holding up? I've only gotten a few scattered reports about what's been going on in Florida these days. Did you ever manage to make it down to the Keys? I think you're right; a small, sparsely populated island with plenty of (working) boats might be the best place to hole up while you wait for all of this to blow over. I'd head for the coast myself, maybe Corpus Christi or one of the smaller towns around there, but that might be a little tricky right now. See, as I write this email on my laptop, I'm pretty much surrounded by the walking dead.

I kind of feel like Butch Cassidy, and these damn corpses are the Bolivian army.

Believe it or not, things actually weren't so bad up until a few days ago. I'd managed to stay hidden and fairly well protected. By the way, speaking of which, thank God I got that cricket bat when I went to that Halloween party as *Shaun of the Dead* a couple years ago, because that thing saved my life more than once, right up until I finally managed to find a gun.

Of course the fact that I had never fired a gun in my life made things a little complicated at the outset, as you can probably guess. I probably looked like an idiot bumbling around that gun shop, trying to figure out what ammo went to which gun. But I did ultimately learn how to work this decent little Glock 9MM I found. It's not the most powerful gun in the world, but it gets the job done, and most importantly, it's simple to use and helpful in close quarters. Can you imagine trying to use a hunting rifle when a zombie is barreling down right on top of you? That's got to be tough.

Living in a second floor apartment was a pain in the ass when I first moved in, trying to get my sofa and bed up that narrow flight of stairs and whatnot, but when it comes to an attack from the living dead, it's a Godsend. It was simple enough to block off the stairwell and obviously they can't reach the windows, seeing as they're about fifteen feet off the ground.

The only tricky part about this setup is getting out, without being noticed, scavenging any supplies I might need. I'm a little shocked that the electricity hasn't completely died. But I have a feeling the grid won't hold up much longer though, which is why I'm okay with going on and on with this email, since it may be the last one I ever write.

That's a depressing thought, isn't it? Imagine all of the trivial emails you've ever sent, and then when you're faced with the prospect of sending one final email, you have to try to cram as much stuff into it as possible, and make it meaningful. I mean hell, this might be the last thing I say to anyone, period. I wish I had some awesomely badass last words, but all I can think of are quotes from people much more clever and witty than I ever could be.

Anyway, where was I again? Oh, right, surrounded. I swear I'm going stir crazy in here, John. I haven't been outside since last Tuesday. Was it Tuesday? God, I don't even know anymore. I've lost track. The apartment is getting stuffy, and I've been forced to put in earplugs in order to get any semblance of sleep to block out the moaning, though my mind has been racing so much with the prospect of death—and the more unfortunate 're-awakening,' so to speak, that accompanies it—that it's tough to drift off and get any rest.

I'm so damn tired. And those inconsiderate, dead bastards outside aren't helping matters with their incessant moaning and groaning. I tell you, zombies are such whiners. We get it already, you want to eat my insides, now just shut up about it, will ya? Let a guy get a little shuteye!

They've been out there for the better part of a week, and more keep coming every day. If those first few had just shut their gaping maws and quit making all that racket, or if I had been able to dispatch them when I had the chance...

I really shouldn't dwell on things like that, but what else do I have to think about? You can only watch so much internet porn before it just gets redundant and annoying, and I think I've watched every DVD in my collection at least ten times since this whole thing started. So now all I think about is what would have happened had I managed to take out those first few ghouls that followed me home from my last little trip outside. I wasn't careful enough, and I just couldn't kill them. God knows I tried, but I couldn't pull the trigger. They were only kids, for God's sake. Maybe ten or eleven years old. I know they're little monsters now, just shells with no souls, but I hope you can understand. They were kids. I couldn't do it. I just couldn't.

So that's what's new in my world. I've got about a week of rations left, about a hundred rounds of ammo, and I'm losing my grip on reality with each passing hour.

On that cheery note, I'm going to end this email. I hope you're doing well, and I really hope you've made it successfully to the Keys and were able to get fortified. If you manage to make it through the winter, you may want to head around up the Atlantic coast, if you possibly can, since hurricane season doesn't care about whether or not you're dodging the undead. Maybe the internet and electricity will still be working, but I doubt it. I'm going to grab some supplies and make a run for it. The window in my bedroom overlooks the covered parking lot, so I think I should be able to hop down and hopefully outrun the dead before they notice me. I'll head for the coast. Maybe I'll find a boat and try to navigate my way across the Gulf and meet up with you.

Here goes nothing. Wish me luck.

Dale

```
Date: 2o July 2010 21:02
From: Trevor <ladies_man34@hotmail.com>
To: Walter <walterTreed@yahoo.com>
CC: David Renfrow
Subject: Party
```

Dude,

What's up, man? How the hell have you been? Man, can you believe this shit? It's the end of the fucking world! How's that song go, oh yeah 'and I feel fine' LOL. Hey, I tried to call you but your phone just keeps going straight to voicemail. What? You don't want to talk to your old frat brothers now? I hope you haven't been bitten by one of those dead things, damn that would suck. You'd be one ugly and hungry zombie, although I can't say anyone would notice a difference, ha!

So get a hold of me as soon as you can, because we are partying tonight! Hey, we better; this may very well be our last night on planet Earth. And if this does turn out to be the end, you better believe I plan on getting drunk and getting laid. Some of the guys are gonna go out and raid a local liquor store and then we're gonna go grab some food somewhere else. We should be back by about ten and then Rachel and some of the sorority sisters are gonna come back around about eleven. I don't think we'll have to worry about the campus PD; they seem to have bigger fish to fry these days. Ha!

So, dude, hit me back when you can, just wanna make sure you aren't dead or walking dead. Ha ha! Plus, I need to know how many people are gonna be at the party. It might be the end, but it would still be rude to run out of food and booze. Okay, dude, let me know. See you at the party to end all parties.

Rock on!

Trevor

```
Date: 19 July 2010 02:42
From: Karen <Kharper@gmail.com>
To: Harry <Hjc36@live.com>
CC: Nelia Thompson
Subject: You were right
```

Dear Harry,
I should have listened to you and skipped this business trip. To start things off, you were right about my boss. He actually thought I would sleep with him to get a promotion. Can you believe that? Don't worry, I told him I was happily married, and to 'fuck off.' After that, he told me the company wasn't gonna pay for my hotel room, and that I would either have to pay for it myself or go home. I opted for home.
I figure when I get there we can call up our lawyer and start a sexual harassment lawsuit. How does that sound? I'm gonna take that self righteous bastard down!
I can't believe this happened. You were right all along. I'm sorry, again, that I didn't listen to you.
Now I'm sitting at the airport, in the middle of the night, and won't be able to get a flight out until tomorrow morning. I'm so very pissed right now. Pissed at him for being such an asshole, and pissed at myself for not seeing it before it was too late.

I'm emailing you from my phone. This place is boring. I suppose I could go to sleep, but I'm still too upset. Besides, the janitor keeps looking at me funny and I'm nervous about going to sleep; you never know what strange people might do.

There are a couple of other people with me in the waiting area, but none of them seem to speak English. They were nice enough to give me a sandwich, though. Apparently they thought ahead and knew to bring food. Everything, and I mean everything, in the airport is closed.

I'm gonna go for a walk. Wanna come with me? Not like you have a choice! Ha ha. I just can't sit still. I need to burn off some adrenaline or something.

I can't wait to see you. I miss you so much! I would love to stretch out in bed with you and press myself up against your side, with my head on your shoulder. *sigh* But I can't, and it's because I was stupid. I don't see how you put up with me, as stubborn as I am! You must love me or something.

I hear some kind of moaning coming from down a side corridor. I wonder if someone's hurt...I better go check it out. Will email again in a bit.

Love ya

Karen

Date: 19 July 2010 03:05
From: Karen <Kharper@gmail.com>
To: Harry <Hjc36@live.com>
CC: Nelia Thompson
Subject: It's me again

Hi

I went to where the moaning came from and there was a man, and he seemed to be hurt pretty bad. There was blood all over the floor around him, and he had a huge

wound on his neck. I kept hollering for help, but no one came. Then he started having trouble breathing! But no one would come and help?
He died. I just watched a man bleed to death! My hands are shaking and I can't stop crying. I don't understand why I'm so upset. It's not like I knew him or anything.
I wish you were here.


```
Date: 19 July 2010 03:14
From: Karen <Kharper@gmail.com>
To: Harry <Hjc36@live.com>
CC: Nelia Thompson
Subject: It's me again
```


He's moving! At least I think I just saw his hand twitch. Do you think it's my imagination? Oh! His eyes just opened. He's not dead after all!
He's sitting up, and looking around. This is weird. Shouldn't he still be hurting or something?


```
Date: 19 July 2010 03:23
From: Karen <Kharper@gmail.com>
To: Harry <Hjc36@live.com>
CC: Nelia Thompson
Subject: I'm hurt!
```


He got a hold of me and tried to bite me...
The fucking bastard bit me! I managed to conk him over the head with a fire extinguisher and he stopped moving again, but he fucking bit me! Can you believe it?
I'm bleeding pretty bad. I have to try to find something to use as a bandage. Stupid me, I left my bag back at the waiting area. Hopefully, it's still there when I get back.

It hurts to walk. I've made it half way back to my bag and I'm taking a break as I type this. Oh shit! The guy is up and moving again! He's stumbling down the passageway, moaning! I have to get moving.


```
Date: 19 July 2010 03:31
From: Karen <Kharper@gmail.com>
To: Harry <Hjc36@live.com>
CC: Nelia Thompson
Subject: I'm scared!
```


I can't make it. I'm now lying in the middle of the corridor, with the light of the waiting area in sight. I can see my bag, but I'm too weak to even crawl over to it, and I'm burning up. I think that guy had some kind of disease. I don't know if I will be able to email you again after I send this one.

He's getting really close to me now. He stopped and is looking at me funny.

Okay, after sniffing me, he grunted and continued down the hall. He's going to the waiting area…

The other people that were waiting with me are now screaming and running away. He must be trying to attack them, too!

I can't keep my eyes open. I hope someone comes and helps me soon. Otherwise, I don't think I'll make it home to you.

If you get this email, call the authorities here and tell them what's going on. You have the list of numbers I gave you, right? I love you so very much! Send help as soon as you can! It might be my only chance!

I love you,

Karen

```
Date: 13 July 2010 9:41
From: Tommy <tlittle@yahoo.co.uk>
To: Carol <CarolineJones@hotmail.com>
CC: Jason D. Brawn
Subject: Please Read This!
```

Hi Carol,

Hope all is well, and you're alive? If you're reading this on your Blackberry, that's great, but I'm running outta time.

How must I explain this to you? I deserve to die. Why? Because I've been a complete swine to you. I've cheated on you numerous times, fleeced money from our joint account, and lied continuously. I don't deserve you and right now, writing this email is worse than those things outside.

I'm sorry and I hope you do survive, and when I become one of them and you see me, please shoot me! That's all!

        Love you always,

            Tommy xxx

```
Date: 13 July 2010 9:49
From: Carol <CarolineJones@hotmail.com>
To: Tommy <tlittle@yahoo.co.uk>
CC: Jason D. Brawn
Subject: Please Read This!
```

Tommy

I tried to call you, but the line was broken. I'm okay. I'm in a church, with many other survivors. We must have got lost in the swarming crowd. Funny how these creatures we used to see, on the big screen, are now roaming the streets of Leicester. I'm not physically hurt. But I am emotionally hurt.
I knew you were cheating on me, and I was gonna slap you with the divorce papers and leave you straight away. This is why I wanted to meet you somewhere remote. But I suppose the zombies got there first.
Anyway, enough of this talk. But please tell me; are you're bitten?

Carol

```
Date: 13 July 2010 9:50
From: Tommy <tlittle@yahoo.co.uk>
To: Carol <CarolineJones@hotmail.com>
CC: Jason D. Brawn
Subject: Please Read This!
```

Carol

Thank God you're safe. I was worried sick about you. No, I'm not bitten. But they are trying to smash their way in. I'm somewhere in a flat above a computer shop. I think it's called Errols. Oh, thank you so much for replying. And please take good care of yourself. Wait a minute. I can see from the window that some zombies are feeding on a shop owner. Oh wow, they're tearing his insides out. There's blood everywhere!
But, tell me something, were you really going to begin divorce proceedings?
If so, I kinda deserved it.
Oh my God, Carol, I'm scared. I'm so scared of going to Hell.

Please forgive me. xxxx

```
Date: 13 July 2010 10:05
From: Carol <CarolineJones@hotmail.com>
To: Tommy <tlittle@yahoo.co.uk>
CC: Jason D. Brawn
Subject: Please Read This!
```

Tommy

You've got to be strong. As for forgiveness. Maybe, you need to forgive me, because I never loved you. I'm so sorry for committing myself in this toxic relationship.

Hope you are still alive to read this.

```
Date: 13 July 2010 10:14
From: Tommy <tlittle@yahoo.co.uk>
To: Carol <CarolineJones@hotmail.com>
CC: Jason D. Brawn
Subject: Please Read This!
```

Carol

Why? Why do this to me now, when you've always said you've loved me? I know you're trying to get back at me, and I fully understand this behavior.

Holy shit, they're coming in. Listen, baby, please forgive me! That's all I need right now!

```
Date: 13 July 2010 10:19
From: Carol <CarolineJones@hotmail.com>
To: Tommy <tlittle@yahoo.co.uk>
CC: Jason D. Brawn
Subject: Please Read This!
```

Tommy

Well, you won't be getting it from me! And if I see you, I will put a bullet in your head, which you so rightfully need!

Oh, I know why you want forgiveness. You want to go to Heaven. Let me tell you something, there is no Heaven or Hell. This is it! This is all you're gonna see. So enjoy what's left, you selfish bastard!
Right now, I'm safe. No zombies in sight. Good riddance to bad rubbish!
      RIP   Carol

Date: 16 July 2010 02:30
From: The Boss <Rockstar80@yahoo.com>
To: webmaster <Daster_D2012@mendent.com>
CC: Michael Bilinski
Subject: The list

Hey,
Hopefully you're still kicking and can post this on my fan website for me. I don't understand any of that programming crap, which is exactly why I hire geeks like you. The tallest gates and widest bodyguards money can buy have kept me safe from those dead things outside, but I'm running dangerously low on the essentials. I figure its time to put my adoring public to work. Don't be a smartass and post this either. You look out for me, and I'll take care of you when this all blows over. Trust me, you'll be knee deep just from my runoff.

Hello everyone,
Over the years you have grown from my fans into friends, and now I truly feel we're all part of a special family connected by the music I've been blessed with the talent to create. It's in the interest of

preserving my abilities for future generations to enjoy that I'm asking for your help in this dark hour.

I know you're suffering. We've all lost loved ones to those flesh-eating abominations roaming our streets. It's easy to give up hope and turn your back on faith at a time like this, but I need you to look deep down into your soul. If you do, I promise you will see this isn't about what I want, but what our Lord wants for me so that I may continue His great work.

I've never asked you (my fans) for anything in the past. I've recorded albums for millions of you to enjoy, and toured our great country so that thousands of you could join me in singing His praises. All the while I selflessly donated a tax deductible 1% of my earnings to the church. Did I ever stop and think about myself?

Just this morning, I took a knee and asked my savior what more I could do. Almost immediately the room filled with a blinding white light, and then I heard the voice. It wasn't stern and booming as some have said, but warm and friendly with just the right hint of age. Kind of like Morgan Freeman in that Jim Carrey movie. It wasn't Morgan Freeman though... It was God Himself.

He bestowed upon me a list. This list contains items that He has asked the truly devoted among you to provide. Before I can share it with you however, there are a couple of things I need to address on His behalf. There are some of you that may raise a suspicious eyebrow while reading these requests. Please remember that He works in mysterious ways and we aren't always meant to understand before you take the role of a Doubting Thomas.

He also acknowledges the risk to life and limb you would be taking by venturing out of the relative safety of your homes. But make no mistake; the current state of affairs is not His work but that of the Adversary. Now, you may be called to lay your life down at the rotted or in some cases skeletal hands of the walking damned. As your intestines are pulled from your abdomen and into the air to be devoured by a ravenous zombie, take solace in the knowledge that you will be met with a handsome reward at the pearly gates.

I will also personally assure that anyone who makes it will be welcome to stay with me at my estate until this zombie business is resolved. So without further ado, here is the complete list as it was dictated to me by the Lord Himself.

1. Women. At lest two at a time, preferably sisters but close friends will do. While our Creator makes people in all shapes and sizes, He stressed that these women be thin, at least a B cup and no older than twenty-five.

2. Alcohol. You can stick to the standards with spirits, but He was very particular about beer. Lager or microbrew only! No malt liquor please.

3. Cocaine. Now I don't know what possible use we would have for this, but He stressed its importance. I suggest bringing as much as you can get your hands on as He wasn't specific about the necessary amount.

4. Food. Pay close attention to this one. Chips, pretzels, frozen pizza or anything on a stick is welcome, but leave the high fiber products at home. It's not like we can just call a plumber.
At this point you may be saying to yourself I don't have some of that stuff, but I know someone who does. Well, you're in luck because He is offering a one time only pass to those of you who steal in order to fulfill one or more of his requests.
Well, I'll let you get to it. Just remember that He loves you and so do I.

The Boss

Date: 22 July 2010 09:35
From: Paul <machineman54@live.com>
To: George <marshall_family@yahoo.com>
CC: David Renfrow
Subject: Need to talk to you

Mom and Dad,

I don't have very much time. We're being moved out at some point tonight. I don't know where we're going, or what we're going to do once we get there. All I know is that yesterday afternoon they called us all together in the mess hall and told us what was going. At first I thought they were kidding, I mean, come on, the dead just don't come back to life for no reason. They told us that at least as far as they can tell, we're safe here on the base.

I was kind of hoping maybe they would just let us stay here on base and protect the civilians who made their way here, but nope. They're going to let the MPs stay here while they send out us infantry units to God knows where. I tried calling you guys a few times, but they confiscated everyone's cell phone and they've turned off the payphones on base.

I guess I just wanted to tell you guys that I love you and to take care of yourselves. If it's as bad out there as they say it is, I don't know what's going to happen. I was talking to one of the civilians who made it here yesterday and he said his group was attacked by about fifty of those damn things. Said they started out with a group of about twenty-five, and by the time the zombies—really, come on—were through with them, their number was cut in half. I didn't really think for one second we would actually be using that word for real someday. Sorry, you know me; I get distracted even during the end of the world. So this guy was telling me he left his neighborhood with twenty-five family and neighbors. All they had to do was make it ten blocks! Ten damn blocks—sorry Mom, I'll tell Father Mahoney about that one if I ever make it to another confession. By the time they got here, there were only twelve of them left! Just twelve! He said they ran into a group of those things, and they just got torn apart! Men, women and little kids just being torn apart and devoured.

You know, I'm kind of glad you guys sent me to church so much when I was little. I feel it's prepared me well for what we're now facing. I really think this is the end. I just wish I knew why, or how. But I guess those questions become irrelevant. Well, I gotta go. I got some guys backing up behind me who want a chance to use the computer while the net is still up. I love you guys, and hope we'll see each other soon. I'll take care of myself; you guys take care of each other. I love you, and thanks for always being there for me.

Your son,
Paul

Date: 12 July 2010 18:17
From: Robert <Robertchassek67@live.com>
To: Sarah <BRabyNone@earthlink.net>
CC: Kevin Millikin
Subject: I just hope you know how sorry I am

Sarah,
It was around two or three in the morning when I ran into the house. I was just happy to be indoors and away from them. Well, at least I thought I was. I wasn't even inside for more than ten minutes, before the first of *them* started flooding into the yard. I think they were following me since the accident. I didn't even have time to grab any food or water from the fridge. Nothing! I've been dying of thirst and I'm hungry!
When I first got here, the zombies weren't all that bad—aside from being dead cannibals of course—so to be safe, I went upstairs into one of the bedrooms and locked the door. I was too afraid to even

move. I hid in a corner until nightfall, when I thought I would be safe—at least to just move around the room—and that's when I'm pretty sure I made the worst possible mistake of my life; I accidentally turned on the light!

I didn't think the power was on anymore. The room lit up like a fucking Christmas tree. I swear to Christ at that moment I heard every goddamn zombie in the Pacific Northwest moan in unison! I quickly turned off the light, but they still made their way up here, and I don't know how they did it. I kept the door closed and remained silent, but they still managed to find me. It's almost like they could smell me.

I've been alone in this room now for... well, I don't know how long. I'm afraid to go near the windows, and I can hear them outside. Finally, the zombies slowly stopped banging on the door. I don't know how much longer I'll be able to hold out. From where I sit, I can see a great deal of damage done to the door frame. Maybe they figured I wasn't inside, and stopped, or maybe the door wouldn't open, and they gave up.

I'm kidding; I know that's not true! If they were going to give up and leave, they wouldn't be outside right now. I've been telling myself that for a couple of hours now, so I feel more optimistic. As I type this email, I can still hear them, all of them. It's maddening, yet I feel my body and mind succumbing to the insanity that comes with their moans, over a prolonged period of time. I hope you're okay, I hope you're alive.

I wish we were together right now. I'm sure we would be, if I didn't run like a damn child. I'm sure, right now that I'm not your most favorite person. Actually, I know I'm not, I heard what you were yelling after the car flipped and I panicked.

"Help me, please help me!"

I want you to know that I'm sorry, I couldn't help it when it happened; I let my fears get the best of me. Have you ever been so scared that when you run, it feels like your entire body goes numb and your legs just take over as if they could sense the nearest safe place to go?

Of course you do.

The world's dead, dying... whatever. We all know what real fear is now, whether we want to or not.

"You asshole, you goddamn asshole!"
I can still hear your voice ringing inside my head, belittling me in my life's final moments. Sometimes I like it because it's of you. Also, your screams let me drown out the sound of the zombies outside my door, pleading for me, but at the same time, I hate it. You're voice will always be there with me until my final breath; reminding me just how horrible I was to the people who really cared for me.
Oh No!
I didn't know the volume was up on my laptop! It's been running on half juice since I started using it. Naturally, the computer's going to die, I just didn't think the battery warning would have been so loud when it warned me. Half of the walking dead in the state of Oregon have to be scratching on my door right now. I know that doors not going to hold much longer.
I think I might just jump out the window. I was looking at it earlier, and now I'm putting more time into the thought. It's not that far down, only one story! If I land right, I can easily make a run for it. Most of the zombies are inside the house anyways.
That's a scary thought! A two-story house filled to the brim with the walking dead, and me. I'm losing my train of thought, my battery time, and I know if I lose that, then I'm losing you. The screen is flashing me a warning—five minutes left of life.
I hope you got out of the wreck and where able to get somewhere safe. I remember seeing we were around some houses when the car flipped, and if I got away, I'm sure you did, too. I hope you did, maybe you're somewhere nearby, hidden in an attic or locked in a basement, and waiting for this email.
I keep thinking about what they did to Suzanne, when they pulled her out of the car, kicking and screaming as they ripped her apart and fed upon her.
I never felt so powerless in my life.
I'd say I prayed to God you got away safely, but after everything I've seen tonight, I don't think He really cares about us anymore, but I do. I hope you're okay. Fuck that, *I know you are*, and I promise you I *will* come and find you.
I need to be able to make things right. I have less than a minute left before the whole thing dies and my email is lost to oblivion. I want

to type some more, because at least when I do, I feel somewhat connected to you.

Any minute now, the door's going to fall, I can see it shaking on its hinges. Pale, bloody fingers are breaking through the boards.

The window's there, and I'm ready to go and make a run for it.

Sarah, I gotta run. This time though, it's not away from you, it's to you. I really hope you get this and remember, I'll see you soon and if I don't, remember, I just hope you know how sorry I am and that I love you.

I always have, always will.
Me

```
Date: 12 July 2010 17:26
From: Sean <Horrorman54@earthlink.com>
To: Gramps <GoldenOlden22@bellsouth.com>
CC: Mike Catalano
Subject: Wanted to say hello.
```

Dear Gramps,

I hope your computer still works. At least they can't destroy the World Wide Web. Remember when I was six years old and I cut my thumb on one of your pocket knives? The blade was so damn small and so sharp that I didn't even feel the slice when it happened. I just glanced at my thumb and noticed blood was gushing out of it. Mom almost kicked your ass for letting me hold the knife. At least we were all eventually able to laugh about the whole incident roughly ten years later!

And I still have the scar to this day! I'm looking at it right now—instead of something else. I don't know why the 'thumb cut' remains such a happy memory for me. Maybe I'm a tad morbid. Or maybe anything that brings me back to the innocence of my childhood—before all this—is a safe bet for peace of mind. Talking to you always helps. I wish you were here to help me right now. You're supposed to burn a knife to sterilize it, right? I think you taught me that once. I've still got the Swiss Army knife you gave me when I graduated from high school. Remember what you wrote on the back?

Keep away from your thumb.

The blade is much bigger on this one and I'm glad. It's definitely helped me out a lot in these new times. I wish I could see you one more time. Yes, I know we agreed to nix all signs of mush, but I've reached a new level of enlightenment, so to speak, which supersedes any initial pacts. Please, don't be mad. You're all I've got left.

I heard screams. I saw a little boy and girl out the window. They were alone on the street. I didn't think. I just grabbed my shotgun and rushed out the front door. I was poised. I didn't see any of 'them' near the children, but knew that one or twenty could be bursting onto the scene at any second.

I reached the boy first, swung the shotgun over my shoulder, and snatched him up. Before picking up the girl, I caught sight of the dead raccoon in her hands; the dead raccoon they were both fighting over. Apparently, the screams of young children don't become altered by 'the change.' I looked back at the little boy just as he took a chunk out of my left forearm.

That happened about twenty-five minutes ago. I know the 'Undead 101' website says you have between fifty and sixty minutes before the infection point explodes and implements full transformation.

All the fingers on my left hand just turned blue—I'm typing the rest of this email with one hand. I just needed to reach out to you as soon as possible to find the strength, the courage, and the mental clarity...

...to use my Swiss Army knife to cut off my own arm. I can't wait any longer and I can't fathom becoming one of them.
Hopefully we'll talk again soon.
I love you.
Sean

Date: 17 July 2010 23:11
From: Cathy <Catherinesummers@live.com>
To: Anita <anitaarmhody@yahoo.com>
CC: Brianna Stoddard
Subject: Are you safe?

Dear Anita,
I have had THE ABSOLUTE WORST NIGHT OF MY LIFE! It started out fine, perfect in fact. Steven took me out to dinner after work, we started drinking, and we came home. He spent hours massaging me and working me up while the champagne continued to flow.
Well, as you can imagine, one thing led to another and we started making the most amazing love I've ever felt! We were enjoying ourselves for a long time before we heard a muffled crash downstairs. Then it went quiet and nothing seemed out of the ordinary so we went back to making love. We kept going for at least half an hour or forty-five minutes with no other noises or distractions in the house. I only thought we'd go downstairs afterwards to find a picture frame knocked down or a book or two knocked off the bookshelf. Steven must have thought the same thing because it didn't give him enough concern to stop what he was doing. You know my husband when he gets going, wink-wink.

Then, when sparks were about to fly for the grand finale, I heard something outside the bedroom door. I told him to hush for a minute because I heard something. We paused and everything got eerie and silent for a split second. Then the door swung open with a big bang and two muscular-looking bikers came in the room. But they weren't normal looking, even for bikers! They were all powdery white and their skin was peeling off their bodies. They were foaming at the mouth and they smelled like rotting corpses. They had the most horrible hunger in their eyes, and they moaned and groaned like imbeciles. Before I could even shriek, they pulled Steven right off me and his penis slipped out rapidly as they pulled him back. Then, I wish I wouldn't have to describe it, they actually ripped him open and they each began eating his organs! I was too shocked to throw up and too terrified to move. My poor husband's dead body thumped onto the floor. I snapped out of it when they turned towards me to single me out for their next victim. I ran like hell out to the spare room and threw a nightgown on and half-jumped, half-ran down the stairs. I was able to grab the car keys and make it out to the car just in time before I became zombie dessert. I soon found out there were a lot of people turning into zombies. They were swarming around the whole town as I plowed through them like a bowling ball through bowling pins. I went to the library and found it crawling with zombies and scattered with bloody victims. I didn't really care how they got there, I just floored it out of there. Then I came to my mother's house where, luckily, she was safe and glad to see me that way, too. I rushed in with her and we re-locked the front door and blocked it with a heavy bookcase. I noticed she had anything and everything around the house blocking windows and doors. I was curious what she had seen and she told me she was attacked by one of them but had escaped. She knew then what was out there.

Now I am here staying with my mother and we're not going to sleep tonight because of this growing epidemic. We must do what we can to survive, however long that may be. Please take care of yourself and let me know if you're all right.

Your best friend, Catherine

P.S.

Try to hide indoors and wait this out. Good luck! I hope you stay safe! I also want you to remember you were always the best friend a person could have. Hopefully that will give you some comfort in these dark hours.

```
Date: 7 July 2010 08:12
From: John <JohnM@medent.com>
To: Max <warvet101@gmail.com>
CC: Anthony Giangregorio
Subject: I need your help!
```

Dear Grandpa,

Mommy and Daddy are dead.

I'm in the attic now, hiding.

The monsters have gotten into the house and I'm so scared. I know I should be brave, after all, I'm almost seven but I can't help it.

When Mommy and Daddy made me come up here, Daddy gave me his laptop. He told me to hold onto it for him.

It was as I climbed into the attic that the monsters came up the stairs.

Mommy screamed and Daddy turned to fight them. He told me to be brave, to not come down no matter what.

Daddy tried to get Mommy to climb the small, fold-down stairs to the attic but she wouldn't leave him.

That was when one of the monsters got by daddy and grabbed Mommy.

I…I try not to think what Mommy looked like as the monster sank its teeth into her neck. I saw Mommy's eyes go wide with pain. But there was something else there, too. Something I don't really understand. It was sadness, I think, the sorrow of knowing she wouldn't get to see me again.

Pretty smart, huh, Grandpa? Mommy says I'm smarter than I should be for my age.

Mommy pushed the ladder closed and told me to stay quiet. That was all I could do, I was so scared. I still am.

Just before the ladder closed and locked me in the attic, I saw Mommy and Daddy surrounded by those monsters, and then the monsters were eating them.

I sat in silence for the next two hours, not moving, not breathing. I could hear the monsters down below, walking around, banging against the walls. The sounds of them feeding made me sick and I almost threw up once, but I remember what Mommy said and I stayed quiet.

When I thought it was safe to move, I crawled to the fold-down ladder. There was a really thin line separating it from the floor. By looking through the line with one eye closed, I could see down below.

I saw Mommy and Daddy but they didn't look like I remembered them.

Mommy had no face, half her scalp was now missing, and Daddy only had one arm, his other in the mouth of another monster. His stomach had been torn open and his insides were hanging out, swinging back and forth as he stumbled around the hallway. I stared at them for almost five minutes and finally I couldn't look anymore.

I cried then, I cried for Mommy and Daddy, and I cried for me, too. I was an orphan now, what was I supposed to do?

I sat there, silent, alone in the attic darkness for almost a half day when I realized the laptop was right there. I used it all the time so couldn't believe I had ignored it. I bet Daddy would have said it was shock I was feeling.

And that's what I'm doing now, Grandpa, I'm emailing you to tell you that I don't know what to do. You told me before that you were in the war. So I need you to come kill the bad monsters—Mommy and Daddy too now—and save me.

I'm hungry now, too, Grandpa, and I have to go to the bathroom. There are no windows up here so I can't see outside, but I can hear the screams of people and the crashes of cars and stuff.
Please come save me,

Your grandson,

Timmy


```
Date: 7 July 2010 09:11
From: Max <warvet101@gmail.com>
To: John <JohnM@medent.com>
CC: Anthony Giangregorio
Subject: Be Brave
```


Dear Timmy,
My heart goes out to you, my daughter-in-law and my son, Timmy. If I wasn't seeing the 'monsters' for myself, I would think you were playing some kind of game with me.
From what you told me, I have to believe my son—your father —is dead and has become one of them. Your father was a good man, Timmy, you should know that, and from what you told me, it looks like he died trying to save your mom, too.
I have some bad news to tell you, son. I'm afraid your grandma is dead. It happened a few hours ago. We were in the kitchen, the house boarded up tight, when one of what you call a monster broke through the barricade on the back door. Grandma tried to stop it from getting in but she was bitten on the back of the hand as she did. She did manage to kill the monster. Your grandma is a tough old woman, and she used a broom to do the job. She spun it around and jabbed the top of it right into the monster's eye, shattering its milky orb and plunging the handle into its brain. It was as she was pulling the broom handle out that the zombie—that's what they're really called— had a little life in it yet and bit her on the back of her hand before dying for good.
We didn't know at the time what would happen, as the news had mentioned it. But I found out soon enough.

First she grew sick, her skin paling to the color of tapioca. Her eyes became sunken in and her lips were pulled back off her gums, making her look like she was grinning. Only this grin was morbid, a sick rictus of a smile that would make any man sick with revulsion.

We had enough time to say our goodbyes, and though she didn't want to die, you should know Timmy, she was okay with it. See, son, me and her have both lived full, long lives and if the good Lord calls us now, we're ready to go.

But not you, Timmy, it's far too early for you to go meet the Lord. When she came back at first I didn't realize it. I was sitting in that old armchair in the bedroom as she slept. The sheets were pulled up to her face and I thought it was so she could shield her eyes from the sunlight seeping behind the curtains. But now I think she just wanted some privacy in her last moments alive on this earth. The low moan was the first sign that she wasn't right. I shifted in my chair and watched as she slowly began to sit up, the sheet slipping off her face and chest. At first I was elated, thinking she was better, but as soon as I saw her face...well, I don't need to tell you all the details. But the pronounced veins spider webbing under her skin, and the way her eyes were glassed over and now a milky white, told me my wife wasn't my wife anymore.

I used the baseball bat I kept in the hall closet—the one you and me used a few times in that field a block from my house—and I killed her with it. I guess I killed her again with it if she was technically dead already.

As I write this to you, Timmy, I'm in the living room; the zombies are still outside and banging on the boarded up windows.

Grandma is upstairs, still in the bed we slept in for over forty years. I covered her up and left her there. It was hard to ignore the blood as it seeped into the sheets and blankets but I closed the door and I don't think I'll be going back in there anytime soon. The place we laid down for sleep, loved and spent so much time together is now her makeshift mausoleum. I wish I could do better for her but it's all I can offer her at this moment in time.

I probably shouldn't be telling you about all this, son, but I feel you need to know the truth. It's the only way you're going to survive the next few days.

You need to stay brave, Timmy, for you won't be alone for long. As soon as I finish this email and hit SEND, I'm going to the basement, getting my double barrel shotgun and my .45, and I'm coming to get you.

You're my only remaining family, Timmy, and I won't let those dead bastards get you, too. They won't take my whole family, I won't let them.

So stay quiet in that attic and wait for me. I don't know how long it will take but I will email you along the way to keep you up to date.

I love you, grandson,

See you soon,
Grandpa

```
Date: 7 July 2010 09:45
From: John <JohnM@medent.com>
To: Max <warvet101@gmail.com
CC: Anthony Giangregorio
Subject: Okay, I'll wait.
```

Grandpa,

I just opened Dad's laptop and saw your email. I'm so glad you got the one I sent.

I will wait for you, Grandpa but I don't know how long that will be. See, the zombies as you told me to call them are getting angry, or it seems like that to me.

They know I'm up here hiding in the attic and I saw Dad trying to get at the string that pulls the fold-down ladder down. It's funny. He doesn't seem like my dad anymore, but somehow he still remembered how to open the ladder, or sort of.

Mom doesn't do much anymore. Since she died, she just walks back and forth in the hallway.

One of the other zombies brought up something bloody and gross. It was eating the stuff and when the zombie reached the rest in the hallway, they all began to fight over it. It looked a lot like raw steak but with bits of tendrils and gross stuff hanging from it. I didn't look too hard as it made me sick. I keep peeking into the small line between the ladder and the floor so I have a good view of them walking around below me. I know a few of them, they're my neighbors. I saw the Stewarts there, both of them. Marge looks pretty bad but Phil only has a small hole in his neck. I liked them because they always let me call them by their first names. They walk around the hallway and act like they don't know my parents, which is weird. They've known each other for years.

I have to go the bathroom now but I'm holding it in. If I can't hold it anymore, I guess I'll have to go on the insulation in the corner. I know my dad would kill me for doing it but seems he's one of the zombies now, I don't think he'll care.

Please hurry, Grandpa. I'm trying to be brave and I want to cry but so far I'm keeping it in. You taught me to be strong, so did Dad, and that's what I'm trying to do. But it's hard, especially with Mom and Dad below me and the way they look.

They look dead but they're still walking around.

Please hurry,

Your grandson,
Timmy

```
Date: 7 July 2010 13:04
From: Max <warvet101@gmail.com>
To: John <JohnM@medent.com>
CC: Anthony Giangregorio
Subject: I'm on my way
```

Dear Timmy,

I'm in my car, parked outside of a Starbucks, using their internet connection so I can email you and let you know what's happening. I hope you're still okay. I pray you are.

It was tough for me to get this far, I'll tell you what. The roads are choked with zombies and stalled cars, fires are everywhere and explosions are common as underground gas lines keep erupting.

It's like a war zone out here.

If I had to guess how long it would take me to reach you, I would have to say I should be there by sunset. So far, I've managed to keep moving in my car. If I have to leave it, well...I don't want to think about that far ahead.

I don't like my chances on foot, I know that.

It was tough leaving my house though. Once I had my shotgun and .45, I went to the back door and pulled off the boards. As sooner as I did this, five of the dead bastards came for me. I shot two in the head and the others I shot in the chest.

I saw the two that got hit in the head stayed down, but the other three were trying to get up pretty quick. I sidestepped them and ran to the garage, and was in my car and leaving before the dead bastards were on their feet again.

That's when I learned it's the head that takes them down for good. Makes sense. No brain, no way to control the body.

But when I got into my car I couldn't believe my bad luck. There was almost no gas. It seemed my now late wife, God rest her soul, hadn't bothered to fill it up.

So the first thing I had to do was go to the gas station.

This proved more difficult with zombies everywhere. I pulled in to the pumps and no one was around. There were a few zombies across the street and I quickly began filling up—thank the Lord for pay-at-the-pump—as they started heading toward me.

It was when the tank was a little more than half full that a zombie came out from behind another parked car at the pumps and sank its teeth into my left arm. Well, Timmy, let me tell you, I was plum scared out of my britches.

he damn thing was gnawing on my arm like it was turkey leg and as it kept chewing and spitting out the material of my shirt, I pulled my .45 and shot it in the head.

Then I checked my arm.

The damn plastic was all scraped up by the zombie's teeth. I tell ya, Timmy, do you have any idea how much a prosthetic arm goes for these days? My veteran's disabilities insurance only goes so far.

As more of the zombies came for me, I topped off the gas tank and jumped back in. I was gone a few seconds later as I watched the stumbling corpses try to follow me in my rearview mirror.

There are a few around my car now as I type this but with just their fists, they can't hurt me. As soon as I'm done with this email, I'll send it to you and get on my way.
Stay safe, Timmy, I'm comin' for ya.

Love Grandpa.


```
Date: 7 July 2010 13:50
From: John <JohnM@medent.com>
To: Max <warvet101@gmail.com>
CC: Anthony Giangregorio
Subject: It's getting bad here
```


Dear Grandpa
I don't know how much longer I'll be safe up here. I'm so scared and I'm crying all the time. It's so hot up here in the attic and I'm so thirsty. I finally went pee in the corner. I had no choice. Now it smells bad up here.
But that's not the worst thing I want to tell you about.
About a half hour ago, the zombies almost got me.
It was Dad. He managed to get the ladder down. As soon as it dropped down, the zombies tried to get up the folding stairs. Luckily for me, they can't seem to really climb that well and the ladder was a tricky obstacle for them. (I learned the word 'obstacle' in school). The zombies still kept trying to climb and finally they just crawled over one another to reach me.
It was my mom that was the first into the attic opening. She didn't look too good, Grandpa. Her skin was so white and her mouth and chin were covered in blood from when she was eating some of that gross stuff that other zombie had brought in earlier. I swear to God, Grandpa, when she looked at me, I almost peed my pants. Her eyes were so dead but yet they were alive, too. There was something in them now, too, something hungry.
Okay, so when Mom began coming into the attic, I knew I couldn't let her, or the ones behind her, so I grabbed the first thing near

me—a plastic Santa Claus. I hit Mom over the head with it and it bounced off her like it was…well, plastic.

With nothing else on hand, I hit her again as she tried to reach out and bite me, and after the second hit, she lost her balance and fell. She struck the zombies behind her and they all fell down to the floor. But Dad wasn't in the group and he began climbing over the bodies to get at me.

I used the rest of the Christmas decorations and pushed them into the opening. They fell down and landed on Dad, covering him with garland and tinsel.

I would have laughed if I wasn't so scared. There was other stuff in the attic so I began pushing it into the hole. Down went the old record player you gave Dad a few years ago, and down went my old box of toys I asked Mom to save for me.

I managed to shove enough stuff into the opening that it's now clogged.

I'm fine now, but there's one thing I should tell you about, Grandpa. I have a cut on my wrist and I don't know how I got it. I think Mom might have bitten me before she fell. Does that mean I'm going to turn into one of them, like Grandma? I don't want to Grandpa, please don't let me turn into one of them.

It's not fair if that happens. That's all, it's just not fair.

I'm going to go now. The battery on my dad's laptop is getting low. I'll check Dad's email account a little later to see if you're almost here to save me.

I love you Grandpa,
Timmy.

```
Date: 7 July 2010 17:44
From: Max <warvet101@gmail.com>
To: John <JohnM@medent.com>
CC: Anthony Giangregorio
Subject: I'm outside!
```

Timmy

I made it Grandson, I'm outside your house!

It was a hard ride here, I'll tell you that. The zombies are everywhere, and the front of my car looks like I drove it through a slaughterhouse. The engine is coated with blood and is smoking something awful. The smell of charred flesh is filling the air around me, making me want to gag as it blows into the vents. But I need the air as it's hot out and I have to keep the windows closed or risk getting attacked.

I'm looking at your house now and I don't like what I see, son. There are zombies everywhere. Your front door is open and they're walking in and out like it's a summer house party.

Oh God, I just saw your mother. She walked outside and stumbled away. Wait, there's your father!

Oh my God, my only son...he's dead. The tears are coming despite my resolve to be strong. I want to go over and hug him but I know that would be a mistake.

Wow, I can't believe it, they're all dead.

Only you remain, Timmy, and as soon as I figure out the best way to get inside your house and kill all the zombies, I'll be right there. I hope you've been safe since your last email, and I hope you've.....

Oh sweet Jesus, oh no, I don't believe it, not you, too.

```
Date: 7 July 2010 18:52
From: Max <warvet101@gmail.com>
To: John <JohnM@medent.com>
CC: Anthony Giangregorio
Subject: Goodbye
```

To my grandson, Timmy,

I'm sending you this email even though I can see you on your front lawn. I'm so sorry, Timmy, I tried to get here as fast as I could. I tried to save you.

Oh, you see me, good, that will make it easier for me to do what I must as your mother and father are also close by.

I'll finish this email in a minute.

Okay, it's done. You, your mother, and your father are now dead with bullets to the head. I can't believe I had the courage to shoot all three of you, especially you, my grandson. But it's for the best. I don't want to think about you wandering around as zombies. And now that you're at rest, we can all meet up in Heaven as I'm sure your grandma is waiting for us.

So this email isn't for you, as you're dead and will never read it. This is for me, so I can leave my last thoughts somewhere. I need to as there's no one else to tell.

See, there's no reason to continue.

No, I'm not a coward and taking suicide isn't an easy way out...not to me anyway On the contrary, I actually find suicide an almost heroic act. To override one's survival instinct and commit the ultimate act is one of strength, courage and resolve.

And I will admit right now, it's easy to be this way when there's nothing left to live for.

I've lived a long life, my grandson. I've served my country but that country is gone, replaced by a land of the dead. My entire family is gone and as far as I know, I'm one of the last few in this state left alive.

Sure, I could try to find other survivors, but for me, at my age, what would be the point? The future is for the young and I'm of the past.

So as soon as I finish this email, I'll send it, and maybe one day someone will read it.

And as my left index finger hits send, my right finger will be wrapped around the trigger of my .45, the barrel in my mouth and angled up so it will penetrate my brain. I try to see the screen as the tears flow freely but it's getting difficult.

Whoever is left alive to read this, I wish you luck in your undead world and know that Max Carlson was a man who loved and was loved, and that in the end, he took the only real option left to him.

SEND

```
Date: 14 July 2010 12:50
From: Janet <janetbaker01@aol.com>
To: Oliver <olliejetting@hotmail.com>
CC: Chelsea Lynn Charters
Subject: Farwell forever
```

My sweet Oliver,
I know you've gone and said your goodbyes already, but it's just not enough for me. I had to write you one last time, before the world is completely infested with death and chaos, and there would be no way to reach you. I've thought about you since the day you left me here, and although I know why you had to leave, it still kills me to know I wasn't your first choice. I know, I know. "Don't

dwell, Janet, I'm not worth the pain." I'll never forget what you said before you boarded that plane for London. You wanted me to move on as easily as you were, but I just couldn't do it. I wasn't strong enough to throw our love away.

But don't you remember? How many times I swore my undying love for you? How sweet my kisses tasted underneath the moonlight in Greenwich Park? Have you forgotten how passionate and deep our lovemaking was? It was so magical and wonderful, and I never dreamed I'd ever experience that type of love. But I did, with you. Oh Oliver, it's all so dreadful. Life is decaying all around me, and as I huddle close to this computer on the cold floor of my apartment, I wish for nothing but you. I don't care if I'm near death, I don't even care that my neighbors and friends have been eaten alive. All I know is that I want you...but I can't have you.

Apart from you being thousands of miles away from me, maybe dead or even one of the infected, I understand that you've lost your adoration for me.

I heard about your recent marriage. Stacey told me a few weeks after it'd happened. You remember her, right? The blonde that worked at the diner near the bookstore? Well, she told me you'd phoned your brother Phil while he was at the diner, giving him details about the ceremony and whatnot. She said he'd told every one in the restaurant the happy news. I'm very happy for you...really. Even if my heart aches at the thought of you with another woman. I'm just glad you've found someone who's good enough to own your heart. It's just too bad I wasn't given the honor.

Hold on, I think I hear one of them. I need to go check...

Never mind, it was a false alarm. I'd heard growling, but it wasn't what I expected; just a lost dog prowling the street below. Anyways, if you're wondering if I've been doing okay during this whole pandemic, I guess I can't complain. Most days I stay holed up in my apartment, with my dresser and couch barricading the front door. I don't think they've figured out I'm hiding up here…but I'm sure they will soon. It only takes one of them to smell you out, then a whole horde appears—they're awfully relentless.

Just the other day, I observed a young woman hiding out in the consignment shop across the street from my building. I'd noticed her before, but never tried to make contact. It would've been too risky. She'd been safe for a few days, but when a few of those monsters went passing by, a bright light flickered through the shop window, almost as if signaling them it was time to eat.

It was horrible. Her screams chilled me to the bone and for the entire hour of their feasting, I didn't dare breathe or move an inch. Soon after they finished with her, they continued on their way, and I was safe once more. Yesterday, I caught sight of her again, roaming around the shop…but she wasn't herself. She's one of *them* now. I don't know what to do. I don't want to die, but I couldn't bear to become one of those *things*.

Remember that gun my father gave me before he passed? The pistol? I'm so glad I have it, so grateful I have a way out. I know that sounds terrible, but I can't stand to live like this any longer. I'm running out of food, and every time I try to go to sleep, I dream up hideous and bloody nightmares.

Sometimes I see you, Oliver. I dream you're still here with me, holding me, helping me forget about this deadly catastrophe. But I've come to the realization that you're never coming back. I'm alone now and alone I will forever be, with nothing but memories of you to keep me warm. When I die, which I've decided will be soon, I won't have any regrets. That's why I had to write you, to tell you how much I still love you. I've always loved you, from the first moment I saw you, and although I'm crying now, don't assume they're tears of unhappiness. I cry in light of the past, when you used to call me yours.

And don't worry about me. I don't blame you, nor do I hate you for deserting me. We all live the paths we choose. I chose to love you forever, but you yearned for more. Besides, I wouldn't trade my memories with you for a life with someone else. You're too special...there's no one like you, Oliver...no one at all.

Now, I think it's time I ended this letter, and I just want you to know that I sealed the rest of my heart within these words. You've always held the other half even if you were unaware...all right, let me try to finish this before I start crying again...

Farewell, Oliver. I pray you're still alive and that you're eyes read this email before I die, maybe then I'll depart in splendid peace. Please don't ever forget how much I love you...and perhaps I'll see you again, not in this life, but the next.

Goodbye forever,
Janet

```
Date: 12 July 2010 18:17
From:  Paul Edwards <paul.edwards@pelaw.com>
To: M.Edwards m.edwards@watersmarketingcorp.com>
CC: Tammy Salyer
Subject: I just hope you know how sorry I am
```

I have no way of knowing if the news is reporting what's going on here, but they've sealed up every building downtown and told us to sit tight until the Guard gets here. Cell towers are either blocked or not working, but we still have power, so I'm writing emails to everyone to let them know that I'm okay. At least for a while. I don't know how to describe what's going on outside, but it's some kind of mass hysteria, rioting and worse. Portland's finest won't tell us anything, and they won't let us leave. But they can't keep us from looking outside.

I wish they could.

Mary, you know I'm not a big believer in crap like the apocalypse, silly end of the world fantasies spread by mentally challenged bible-beaters like your Uncle Carl, but if you could see what I've been seeing these last few hours…what can I say? There may be something to it. There are people out there that look like they've been through a garbage disposal and came out the wrong end, but they're still vertical, still *mobile* even. And that's just the beginning. They're sick, obviously sick, and they've got some kind of dementia that's making them act, the best I can describe it is, like an animal. Inhuman. They're just going around killing everyone unlucky enough not to be able to outrun them.

I watched Judge Blake get attacked by twelve jurors who were coming in for today's trial. All twelve of them rushed him like a football team. He saw them coming and started to run inside, but his robes got all twisted around his legs and he tripped on the back stairs. They were on him like he was some sort of meat buffet. I won't tell you what else I saw, but that should be enough to make you see why I'm starting to relax a little on my beliefs about the end of the world.

I don't know how things are going to turn out, but I feel like I should tell you something. I'm not sure I'll ever get another chance.

Mary, I've always hated you.

I never told you, but I've wanted to. I spent hundreds of long nights—three years worth, each and every night—thinking of all kinds of ways to tell you. A letter that I wiped my ass with, a bouquet of black roses and a note, or maybe a singing telegram. None of them seemed good enough, *potent* enough, to really get the message across to you. But I never in a million years thought I'd be telling you through an email while half of Portland is trying to hunt down and kill the other half.

I know you'll say it's pathetic. I could be just a few hours from dying and all I can think about is telling you how much I loathe you. Being a divorce attorney, you'd think it would have come easily to me, but I've kept it bottled up for so long that I don't think I could stand to die without you knowing.

All those times you said you wanted a divorce and this is it, finally, our definitive end. There'll be no divorce now, so you can shove all those accusations of adultery and threats of alimony suits right up your ass. That is, if you can unpucker it long enough.

What the hell were we thinking? Two people with ambition, lucrative careers and overlapping social circles does *not* a match in Heaven make. For God's sake, you could barely stand the sight of me before I even slipped the ring on your finger!

Can you blame me for going to Acapulco with that blond honey from your marketing department? And let's not pretend you didn't have your share of beefcake during these last couple of years, too. Just because I never caught you *in flagrante delicto* doesn't mean I didn't know it was happening. I saw some of those overly muscled, silicon pec'd behemoths at Gold's Gym, the ones you had to put in 'extra' training time with so you could keep your middle-age spread at bay. I know that's not all you were spreading, sweetie pie. I may be an ass, but I'm not stupid.

Take it from me, based on some of the shit I've seen today, you can bet those boys aren't looking quite so good anymore.

I was happy to see you go to Dallas for another conference this week, but now I'm wondering if maybe it would have been better if you'd stayed here. If I live through this, I'll still be cursed with having to wake up every morning to the stench of you drowning yourself in that hideous White Diamonds perfume, and I'll still have to listen to that disgusting gargling noise you make after you brush your teeth. You sound like a goddamned choking mule when you do that. You always said you wanted more honesty in our relationship. I hope you're happy, darling, because I'm finally stepping up to your obscenely high expectations.

A horrible thought just occurred to me, maybe this outbreak has hit Dallas, too. Jesus, you might not even get this email. That would be a fucking joke.

There's something going on downstairs, I hear screaming, so I have to end this. I want you to know how much better I feel for finally telling you the truth. And if you get this email, you can consider our marriage over. Life's too short.

Paul

Date: 19 July 2010 12:52
From: George <Toomraider@gmail.com>
To: Chris <ChrisDellmont_gg@yahoo.com>
CC: Anthony Giangregorio
Subject: Wanted to tell you something

Dear Chris,

I know you won't ever read this email, because as I look out my window, I can see you on your front walkway getting eaten by zombies.

Still, I can't help but want to send this last email to you for the hell of it. Hey, I have nothing do, as I'm trapped in my house.

See, I wanted to tell you what an asshole you are and that I fucked your wife.

Yup, did her for almost two months every day when you went to work.

It wasn't an emotional thing, purely sexual. She said you didn't please her and I guess she was looking for something on the side. And that's where I came in.

You remember that time I let you borrow my lawn mower and you gave it back with no gas and a broken front wheel? Well, I do. And how 'bout the time I let you use my hedge clippers and you gave then back all rusty after leaving them in your backyard in the rain? They're still pitted to this day, you jerk.

So when your wife started coming on to me, I couldn't say no, hell, I loved it. She's quite a hot piece of ass, Cindy is, or she was until that pack of zombies ripped her face off a few minutes ago.

I don't know why you didn't board up your doors and windows like they said to on TV. You made it so easy for those dead bastards to get at you.

Oh, well, live and learn, I always say.

After I send this email to you, I'm gonna get my shotgun, stick it out my second floor bedroom window, and wait for you to come back from the dead. I just peeked out the window and it looks like the zombies are gonna leave more than enough for that to happen, too. I only see one arm missing and though your insides have been torn out, we both know you won't need them anymore anyway.

Your wife didn't fare as well, I'm afraid. It looks like she won't be coming back. They tore off her damn head! Wow, that's cold. Her mouth is still moving up and down and her tongue is hanging out, or it was until a pale hand tore it from her jaw. Damn, those things are strong. They were fighting over her insides like she was a piñata. A couple were playing tug of war with her intestines, well, they were till it snapped, sending both falling on their undead asses!

Okay, it looks like I'm ready to finish this email as I just saw you begin to stir.

I've been looking forward to this for a longtime, and now that you're a zombie, it's all nice and legal.

See you in Hell, Chris my boy, dress light, I hear it's warm down there!

Your ex-neighbor,
George

```
Date: 23 July 2010 19:23
From: Jane <BloomingRose@EAHS.mail.edu>
To: Paul <EAHS_QB2010@EAHS.mail.edu>
CC: Matt Leverton
Subject: Update
```

Dear Paul,

I know it has been a few days since my last email. I'm not even sure you're getting these anymore. I know now there isn't any escape. Those *things* are everywhere. I can hear them in the night, scratching at the walls and scraping their bony fingers against the bricks. Chelsea is gone, so are Roger and Bill. Chelsea was stupid; I wish I could have told her so. No one ever thinks the coast is clear and sticks their head out the window. One of those bastards grabbed her by her scalp, it made a loud tearing noise, but her screams overrode it. Her screams didn't last long. I hope mine don't…

It kills me to think we'll never be married. To think this goddamned dorm room will be my mausoleum. I should have stayed home and went to state.

If you get this, please know how much I love you. I know now that there is no cavalry coming to save me or anyone else. The gunfire stopped about a week ago. Instead of taking those things out, we're just skirting around the place, hoping they don't hear us. As I said before, Bill and Roger are gone. I can only assume they're dead. They left one night and never returned. The girl from down the hall, Dawn, is still here. She babbles from time to time, about hearing those things outside.

Should I call them zombies? Undead? Living Dead? Hell's Rejects? I don't really need a name for them.

Why did this happen? Why couldn't we have been together when the outbreak occurred? I would give anything to feel your hands on my skin again.

Remember last Halloween? The children laughing in the streets dressed in pretend costumes of bloodsucking beings, eating candy… These days the kids I see are still in the streets sucking the bones of their victims like feral dogs.

We have no weapons anymore, I'm guessing we have a curling iron or something around here, something to use as a flail if need be, but it'll do little damage if more than one come in.

I don't know which I can't stand more. Dawn's whining and babbling about the end coming or the moaning dead just three floors below. The doors are barricaded but I know it's just a matter of time.

I heard a crash a second ago, and when I looked over at Dawn, I saw she was gone; she'd jumped out the window. I guess I should be shocked, but I'm not. Now I'm alone on this entire floor. I guess I'm more terrified than anything. I guess Dawn got tired of babbling, and decided to end it all. There's blood everywhere; she must have cut herself on the glass as she went through it.

It'll be dark soon and I can feel them all around me even two stories down. I know they'll eat me, I know they'll enjoy and be sated for a short while, but I can't help but wonder how I'll get out of here. Until the jaws clench down on me, I still hope to get out of here…

Two all beef patties…special sauce…

God, I'd kill for a Big Mac right now. We've had to resort to rationing food. We hoped Bill and Roger would come back with supplies, but I guess that's a lost cause. If I wasn't afraid of becoming infected, I'd cook those dead bastards, the few that caught on fire smell absolutely delicious, like roasted pork.

I'm tired. I need to close my eyes now. The moaning and scraping of fingernails on wood is too much. I love you, more than you'll ever know. I just wish things could have been different. Do you think there's still a Heaven? If so, maybe we'll meet up there. That would be something.

Above all, I just wish I could get one word back from you.

All my love,

Jane

```
Date: 2 July 2010 11:32
From: Tom <truckerman@yahoo.com>
To: Jenny <lilwoman24@gmc.com@live.com>
CC: Nelia Thompson
Subject: You deserve better
```

Dear Jenny,

Oh, darling, I've really done it this time. I've messed up bad. I'm scared to tell you what I've done. But I'm sick because of it, and I think this will be the last time I'll ever get to talk to you.

It all started when I was at a truck stop a few miles back. I can't even tell you how far, because I got so scared.

I was horny, so I started looking for a prostitute. I know I swore to you I would never cheat on you again, but I was weak. I'm so sorry, babe. If I'd kept my promise, if I'd been a good man to you, none of this would be happening right now.

I found one. The Lot Lizard was peddling herself at the truck stop, and stupid, asshole me, picked her up. Again, I'm terribly sorry. Please don't stop reading this. I need you to know what happened. I really do love you, despite my shortcomings.

Well, she seemed a little messed up when she got in the truck, and while we were…

Anyway, she died! I mean, right in the middle of it! It really freaked me out. I didn't know what to do. I was thinking about just dumping the body, I mean, who would ever trace it back to me. I planned to drive for a while and then dump her along the side of the road. I know, I'm such an asshole.

While I was driving, she started moving around again, and moaning. I nearly ran off the road, it scared me so bad. I managed to pull off onto the shoulder, and by that time she was sitting up. I asked her if she was okay, told her I would pay her and leave her off at the next truck stop, but she didn't respond. She just kept moaning and groaning.

I crawled into the back, to the bed where she was still just sitting there. She didn't look right, there was something strange about her eyes and the way she was moving. That's when I noticed a wound on her ankle. It looked like a bite, like something had torn out a chunk of her skin off. I wished I hadn't been thinking with my little head and had noticed that sooner.

I tried talking to her again, and she snarled and bit my hand. I was pretty pissed. I opened the door and shoved her ass out. She tried to climb back in and bite me again. We had quite a tussle!

After I drove away, she walked out into the middle of the highway and I saw her get run down by a car. She flew through the air, the car came to a screeching halt, and she got back up and attacked the driver that got out to see if she was okay. She ripped the driver's throat out with her teeth.

I drove and drove, not really paying attention to where I was going. It's a good thing the company installed the GPS units in all the trucks. I just did what it told me and kept on driving.

It was only a matter of hours before I started feeling sick–a fever and an upset stomach. I knew I needed to take a break, so I pulled into the next town I came upon. I'm emailing you from there. They have an internet café.

I don't know what was wrong with that whore, but I think she was a zombie. I know that sounds crazy, but there's no other explanation for it. What else would come back from the dead and then want to eat people? A vampire? I'm leaning more toward the zombie, because of how she looked, and the way she moved, and about all that stuff they've been saying on the radio about people attacking people.

But I've been bitten, so it's only a matter of time before I'll become a monster, too. I'm burning up, and I can smell the people around me. Not like they stink, but I can smell them like when you catch the aroma of a steak grilling and your mouth starts watering in anticipation.

I'm getting weaker, and I know I won't be 'me' for much longer. I'm sorry again for cheating on you. I wish I had been a better man, one you deserved.

Tell the kids I love them.

Always remember that I love you.

Tom

Date: July 2010 11:26
From: Gerald <Bago87pt@earthlink.net>
To: Johnny <hotrodsrcool@gmail.com>
CC: David French
Subject: Where are you?

Hey Johnny,
For now, the power's on and I say thank you to the brave guys at the power plant!
I'm sorry I didn't reply to your last email. I really wish I had. We always think there will be time enough tomorrow, but I don't know how many more tomorrows there will be. When the power goes off the next time, I don't think it'll come back on, so I'm writing this as fast as I can.
I'm here at our granddad's old farmhouse writing you in the hope you and your family are okay!
If you get this email and you're able to get here, then get here as fast as you can! I need to know that my big brother and his family are safe.
Just a warning I-64 and I-95 are war zones, so take the back roads and don't trust anyone!
You should have been here yesterday, Johnny, it was a blast, I mean it!
The zombies or the undead or whatever you want to call them came at us enmass. They must have come from Richmond. It's burning as I write.
They arrived just before sunrise yesterday!

We were caught off guard, as many of us have become complacent after not seeing the zombies in any numbers for a while

We built a small pill box on the roof of the farmhouse and the two guys in it woke us with the first shots over what had been the corn field out back.

The old barn has been reinforced and turned into a bunker, and the guys in it opened up with two S.A.Ws and at least four M4s, just like the ones I used during the Gulf War.

Even as dark as it was, I could see dozens of zombies being ripped to pieces from the thousands of 5.56 mm rounds that filled the old corn field with hellfire and brimstone.

Bill Evans and I took up sniper positions on the roof over the kitchen and tried to make every shot a head shot.

By early afternoon, we had things under control as we stacked and burned the bloody and filthy bodies from the field.

Many of the zombie bastards were missing arms and legs and had to be finished with a .22 bullet to the head before we could drag them away.

Some were slow, but a lot of them were fast enough to make it to the back of the stable where we keep the horses, and thank God none of the horses were harmed. We need the horses for transporting supplies and scouting the area around the farm. The gas powered vehicles are there for our escape if it should come to that.

 Lewis Johnston was our latest fatality, I know you remember him. He kicked your ass when you started dating his sister back in high school. Well, he went to check the corn field for any bodies we may have overlooked yesterday and he got bit on the ankle.

A few of the women have set up a clinic in one of the backrooms of the farmhouse. They cut Lewis' foot off trying to save him, but the bleeding never stopped.

I just heard a shot fired from Lewis' room, so I ran to the room to see what happened. He'd died and gone over! One of the women had to shoot him, may he rest in peace!
 Well brother I'll set a place for you at the table and if I don't see you again in this world, then I'll look for you in the next.

Much Love,
Gerald

Date: 17 July 2010 11:37
From: Robert <Robconstrat88@hotmail.com>
To: Jamie <Jamitrudin_DD@yahoo.com>
CC: Alan Spencer
Subject: The break-up

Jamie,
There's not many guys who can say they proposed to their girlfriends just days before the dead came back to life. And there's not very many guys who can say they were turned down either. Seriously, Jamie, did you ever think about the scenario, 'If I was the last man on Earth,' because I very well could be the last 'living' man on Earth any day now. We're being slaughtered left and right. I watched my best friend drive to my house from my bedroom window on his motorcycle. Davie was the brave kind; he'd weave around those pus bags, playing games, but one of them lifted up their arm and clothes-lined him. Snapped his neck, and lucky for him, he was dead, but they peeled off his helmet and ate him up until there was nothing left but street pizza.

Imagine, my best friend since childhood risks and loses his life to see if I'm okay, and you don't even return my calls, my texts, and now, my emails. We dated for six years; doesn't that mean anything to you? I was there when your mother died of breast cancer. I baby-sat your little brother on our 'dates' to help your dad out. I'm a good man, and you're so unwilling to just talk to me is driving me crazy.

I know what the problem is; it's Deke, isn't it? You're screwing him. You've been fucking him. Big-dick Deke.

I called Shannon, Cat, Linsey, and all your stupid whore friends, and they told me you were bored with me. They said I was smothering you, and it was getting annoying. You wanted a fling. Some fun. "A dick without repercussions," Cat said.

Well, I guess you're having a lot of fun alone, because I saw Deke's Jeep Wrangler crashed in a ditch about two hours ago. I went to the trouble of trying to save him, to show you I still care. And you know what? He's one of them now. He shambled after me from the woods with half his throat eaten up and his heart exposed in his chest. So I shot him in the head, like all the radio reports keep saying to do. His entire face disintegrated! My .45 pistol erased that shit-eating grin off his face, that goddamn cutie pie face you found better than mine.

Now it's melted cheese!

I'd protect you through this. You know I love you. I always will. We're soul mates. You'll come around, honey. I can feel it. I'll never give up on us. You will be my wife, and we'll have those two perfect kids, the house, the picket fence, and no dogs, seems you like cats. We'll have plenty of cats. An orange one, if you want. It doesn't matter. I'll change. I'll be spontaneous. I won't smother you. I'll act like I don't care when you want me to, and I'll act like I care when you do. Anything, baby, just to make you happy.

Maybe I'll be the only one left soon enough, seriously. Judging by all the ransacked houses and streets of wrecked cars and the walking dead every-where, it's Armageddon time. The great Big Judgment; God's wraith for not keeping the tithing baskets full, or maybe we didn't read the Bible enough. "The quota for scripture reading wasn't met this year, folks, so I'll smite you with the living dead." Who knows what the fuck is really going on?

It's funny when girls break up with boys, I've been thinking. Women always have a contingency plan. A literal pulling of the ripcord. You were going to go on a trip the day after you left me for Deke. That Jeep was full of camping gear. I'd be crying my eyes out, and you'd be home free, and I'd have no way of getting in contact with you. That's a bitch thing to do. A cold-hearted bitch thing to do, you know that?

But no worries. I'm almost to your house. I'm bleeding, but again, no worries. I'm not bitten. You see, I'm sitting in your younger brother's clubhouse outside in your backyard, writing on my laptop. Wireless service still works, but the battery is almost dead.

Your dad's a good shot, by the way. Are you wondering why you heard a bunch of gunshots and then silence? It's been about ten minutes. He hit me with that puny-ass .22 rifle in the shoulder. Only grazed it, lucky for me. Unlucky for him, I shot him right between the eyes. He didn't even call out to ask me if I was one of them, but just opened fire on me like he wanted me dead either way.

Did you tell him to shoot at me, Jamie? I'll give you the benefit of the doubt. It was an accident he shot me, and it was an accident I blew his goddamn brains out.

I guess we're Even Stevens.

We're going to have good times; really revive those romantic juices between us. It's been five weeks we haven't touched each other. When the power goes out and we light up those candles, can you imagine? Once the bleeding from my shoulder slows down, I'm going to crawl up that gutter pipe and into your old bedroom window like I did when we were dating in high school, and we'll finally be together again.

I can't wait to hash things out, honey.

I'll always love you.

Robert, your husband to be.

```
Date: 7 July 2010 9:41
From: Gwen <AlistairandGwenHall@hotmail.com>
To: Michael <Michealthall@FBMidbank.com>
CC: Sean T. Page
Subject: My first email
```

Dear son,

I hope Debbie and the kids are keeping well. I think you'll be impressed by my first email, it's true, your old mum is finally wired up on the interweb.

I hope city life is treating you well. Please take care of yourself, it's a stressful job and remember, Mr. McKay said that the position working on the island ferry is open as long as you want it.

Well strange things have been happening on the island since my last letter–did you get that one? It included the stuff on Muriel's wedding–a very uncouth affair. Uncle Angus got drunk as skunk but this time it all went too far. He punched the priest and then got into a truck with David McFarlane, you remember, the policeman whose mum used to work at the video shop.

Anyway, back to events on the island. Firstly, we've had no tourists for the last few weeks, suppose it's the health crisis, people afraid to travel, that kind of thing. So, it's been quiet, really quiet– never thought I'd miss the mainlanders that much....

Then yesterday, the health centre at Murray Lock 'disappeared.' I say disappeared, its still there, just cut off. The RAF are there but the whole place is sealed off. Pa tried to pick up my angina tablets and was rudely hassled away. The way they treated him was a disgrace. He told them he was a former guard in the Black Watch; it cut no mustard with those chaps. One of them, a Londoner of some sort just said "Look why don't you just piss off, Granddad while you still can."

Needless to say, a letter will be on its way to Major McCloud. I just wish Pa had taken down their unit numbers.

There was a knock on the door a few minutes ago. It was Letty from the Post Office. There's no travel on or off the island. We're cut off! Can you believe it, last time was the great storm of 1965. Remember that, when Pa's plastic greenhouse blew away? I think you were only about two at the time.

We just had an interruption in the electricity. Means we're on island power now, wind power from the turbines. Still, at least it helps cut down on the oxygen in the atmosphere. You know even in our little community, we like to do our bit to stop greenhouse warming.

Your Pa's just returned as well. He was going to put his gun on the shelf but I yelled at him. I can't have that mess everywhere again; the grease took me weeks to get off last time.

Son, things are very queer here. Pa went back outside and is locking the main gates. When he came in he was all over the place, bright red his face, you know how he gets. I said you're going to have a heart attack Alistair Fraser Hall, but he just dashed over and started loading the gun.

I just tried the phone before I started writing this but it's not working. I don't even know if the interweb is still working. I checked Google and it's still on. I searched for highland gardening, over twenty million hits–something for later I think.

So, Pa and I are now locked in the cottage. He's closed the shutters on the downstairs window. It's all rather fun really, reminds me of the safety training we did during the war. I don't know if old Mrs. O' Sullivan is all right. Pa said we all had to stay indoors. There might be some murderers on the loose. To be honest, it's all very exciting. Biggest thing to happen on the island since young Bobby Keith crashed the ferry in 1994.

Ah Michael, I don't know how to tell you this but Pa, I think he's almost killed someone. A man was staggering up the front path. Pa warned him, he really shouted but the chap just kept on coming. Pa opened the window in the bathroom and shot the man in the shoulder, I think. Now the man is just lying there, grumbling. The phone isn't working so we can't report a thing. Also, as the gun recoiled, Pa stepped back and put his foot right down into the toilet. As he fell back, he twisted his ankle very badly. He's in the front room at the moment with a bag of frozen peas on his leg.

I daren't go and check on our intruder–he might have his way with me! Pa said we need to sit tight until the authorities arrive. That's what we're going to do. It was self-defense anyway—they can't put a man in prison for that, can they?
I'll write back more a little later.
Love you lots,
Mum

Date: 7 July 2010 15:36
From: Gwen <AlistairandGwenHall@hotmail.com>
To: Michael <Michealthall@FBMidbank.com>
CC: Sean T. Page
Subject: My second email

Hello again, son, I didn't realize the computer was only on sleep, it's been six hours since I last updated this but I want to tell you a few more things.
I've seen loads of folks staggering around, they must have looted the Skye Whisky Brewery as they look drunker than Uncle Angus gets at funerals. With Pa crippled, I'm really a woman alone so I'm just keeping quiet. A backpacker approached the house about an hour ago so I just pretended not to be in and he eventually went away, but not before he hammered on the door for about an hour, moaning and groaning. I bet he was from down south; I don't know what it is with those people, in too much of a rush if you ask me.
I don't know what's happening now Michael; I do wish you were here. About ten minutes ago a police car came flying round the corner and into our fence. Then an officer, I think it was PC McDuff, came running up to the front door. I quickly opened it for him. I half-thought it was some awful news of a terrorist attack in London or something, he knows you're down there working. But he was covered in blood. He almost fell in the doorway.
Pa tried to get up but couldn't–he's now under about five pounds of frozen vegetables. Well, all of sudden, I notice a strange look in

PC McDuff's eyes, a sort of yellow tinge. I tried to sit him down with some tea, that usually does the trick but he became really quite agitated. He started waving his arms around, banging into things and he broke Auntie Lille's clock, the one from Edinburgh. That's when I saw the bite on his arm at the wrist.

Anyway, he was soon joined by another officer, the new one, I don't know his name, surly sort of ferrety chap from Glasgow, and all hell broke loose.

They attacked your Pa!

I tried to get to him to help, I really did, but I couldn't reach him. They were right over him, biting him, clawing him. I tried to hit one with a walking stick, but they just carried on. I panicked and ran into the office and latched the door.

I can still hear them hammering on the door. Now I'm glad Pa didn't adjust the door as I can see through the inch gap at the bottom.

When I peeked, I saw Pa's faded red gardening socks through the gap. They must have sorted something out. I think we should be in line for some compensation after this. The garden's a write-off thanks to the police car in it. They're still banging and moaning or talking really low, I suppose.

I'll go back and see how everyone is doing in a moment.

But first I'll get this email sent off.

I just looked out the window, it's gray, very gray, looks like we're in for another one of those storms. What was it old Mrs. O' Sullivan used to call them? 'End of the world' she used to say. Grim old character. I hope she's all right.

I'll let you know how we get on here in my next email. Now that I have the hang of it, it's kind of fun. I'm sure Pa won't be walking properly for at least a month with that ankle, not to mention what the two officers did to him!

Take care and know that we love you,

Mum

```
Date: 20 July 2010 13:27
From: Simon <senorcaco@hotmail.com>
To: Liz <LJ.V@Harmonious.com>
CC: Chris Deal
Subject: Miss you
```

Liz,

Babe, are you all right? I keep calling your cell, but I can't get through. I tried your landline, too, but I think they're down up there. Damn near everyone must be trying to call someone, I guess. The lights were flickering when I woke up, but the power seems to be holding for now, and at least the internet is still up. Do you know what's going on? Everything was fine last night.

Ed and I, we went out for a few pints and when we came home the streets, well, they were quieter than normal, but nothing weird. Now it's madness out there.

That's all I can think to call it, babe, madness.

Like I said, when I woke up to get ready for work, the lights were flickering. It took a little longer for the water to warm up for my shower, but beyond that, everything seemed fine. I was a bit hung-over, but nothing seemed out of the ordinary.

When I went downstairs, I could hear a siren going on. I figured there was a wreck out on Sam Furr, like there always is this time of day. I parked out on the strip last night. There weren't any cars out there, and I came out the door between that Tapas restaurant I live over and that kid's clothing place. Outside, that's where the madness was. Bodies all over the ground, some still twitching. Cars stopped in the middle of the road, the drivers gone. That siren was coming from an abandoned cruiser, the door swinging on the breeze and a handprint of blood on the passenger side window. The doors and windows of the Starbucks across the way were broken and shattered. There was this smell in the air, and I couldn't place it; all I knew was it was wrong.

That's when I saw them.

A group loitering on the corner, like the kids normally do in the summer, with nothing else to do but come down here and stand around. They saw me, the group, maybe twenty of them just standing there, and when they turned, I realized what was wrong.

Blood covered the front of their clothes. Bullet holes in their chests. Arms and legs at odd angles. They were dead. I can't for the life of me explain why or how, but they were dead and they were coming toward me, a slow shuffle, barely a pace at a time, but they kept coming and more were joining them from the broken windows and doors of the shops and restaurants, some getting up from the ground.

A constant moan like something out of Hell was all I could hear, blocking out even the siren.

It took a few moments, one or two beats, for me to realize I was just standing there, watching them get closer. Several of them had broken fingers, exposed bone that looked like it would work well in ripping me apart.

Their eyes, dead glassy orbs, were fixed on me with something like hunger burning where there minds used to be, their souls.

When I realized they were more than willing to kill me, that they were going to eat me if they got within biting distance, I turned, dropping my briefcase, and ran up the stairs to the apartment entrance. I took the stairs three at a time and I pulled hard on the door, but it wouldn't budge.

The code. I always forget about that.

I pressed 5-1-3-9 on the keypad and the door opened with a buzz. I slammed it closed as the first one got to the stairs. Through the safety glass, I watched as they came toward me, no hands going to the handle, just body after body slamming against the metal door, slapping weakly against the small glass window in the center of it. The door held, and the frame showed no signs of budging. The landlord installed good locks after that rash of break-ins last year. I ran back up to my apartment and locked myself in. First I tried the phone, trying to see if I could get through to the police. No dice. I tried calling you, nothing, then my parents...again, not a damn thing. I called work, and it actually went through, but I stopped waiting for an answer after fifteen rings. I went to the balcony and looked out. From one end of the complex to the other, I could see nothing but those damned things, moving slowly like drunks, from one side to the other, some coming out the main entrance onto Sam Furr, some heading to the subdevelopment behind us.

If it's as insane where you are as it is up here, I'd hate to know what it's looking like over there. Could anyone get out? Would those things block the roads? There's hardly any room to maneuver on a normal day, let alone now.

I hate to even tell you this, considering how long you tried to get me to quit, but I sat out on the balcony for a while having a smoke. I stashed a pack for a day when I knew I'd need one and I went through five before my hands stopped shaking.

I'm sorry, you know. If I can't get out of here, if I can't see you again, I want you to know I'm sorry that I'm not the man you needed me to be. I could have been better for you. I should have been.

All I can hope is that up there on the lake you guys are fine. If it got crazy, hopefully you went out on the boat, just sat in the middle of the water until things mellowed out. The television is just repeating the same thing over and over: "Stay in your homes. Try and keep all contact to a minimum." They aren't even telling us what's going on. You think it had something to do with the nuclear plant? I knew back in college when we protested that place it would be the end of us. I don't know if I'd prefer a Chernobyl situation to this. Fallout and radiation poisoning. You know, I think I recognized a couple of those things that came after me. I'm pretty sure one of them was that barista at the Starbucks who always hooked us up with free refills.

The television says to stay home and not to go outside. While I was out on the balcony, I saw that if I could make it to my car, if I jumped the curb, I could make it out of the complex. The interstate is just one streetlight up, and it can't be that bad, could it? Could I make it up to you?

I tried calling you again. It still won't go through.

You know what? I have to try. I'm coming up to you. I've got that old baseball bat in my closet, it ought to be able to put some of them down. If I can get an opening, I'm going to go see if the abandoned police cruiser has anything in it I can use. A shotgun maybe, or some body armor.

Those things aren't at my door any more, at least I don't hear them. This is as good a time as any to run for it, I guess. Hopefully I'll see you soon. If you're there, we'll go out on the lake and wait it out. Enjoy some sun, the breeze. I never did get a chance to kiss you out there on the water. Wish me luck.

I love you,

Simon

```
Date: 22 July 2010 09:35
From: Mike <mickeydollen@Juno.com>
To: Tara <taramitchell99@yahoo.com>
CC: David Renfrow
Subject: Wanted to check in with you
```

Dear Tara,

Hey it's me. How's my favorite girl doing at school? I guess you know what's going on. They probably aren't able to totally shut you guys off from the world at that little tiny school you go to, so you probably know all about the dead coming back to life. I hope you're safe, and holed up somewhere deep in the bowels of a basement or something. I tried calling you a bunch of times, but cell service is terrible right now, and when I tried to call that other number you gave me, it just rang and rang.

So like I said, I hope you're safe. If anyone you're with has been bitten by one of those things, get away from them as fast as you can. Based on what I've seen, they won't last long anyway and they will attack anyone around them. You probably know all this, remember the countless Halloweens we spent watching bad horror movies and laughing at how ridiculous they were? Well, this isn't some bad movie, if you haven't seen one yet, this is really happening.

All right, so you probably want to know why I'm emailing you. You're tough, you're a survivor. I'm going to try to get to you, but I don't know what's going to happen. They say the roads are jammed and even if you survive the zombies, there are already gangs of people out there robbing and raping. Ah, don't you just love how a catastrophe brings out the best in the human race? It normally takes me three hours to get to your school on a good day, well let's just say that today is anything but a good day and I don't know how long it will take me. Just hang on, if you get this, stay safe and know I'm trying as hard as I can to get to you.

One more thing. You and I have been friends since middle school. All the vacations our families went on together, and all the holidays spent so close to one another. Those were some of the best memories of my entire life. If this is the last thing I ever get to tell you, well, I just want to say that I love you. Yeah that's right, I said it. I have loved you for a long time, and I pray I'll get to tell you in person. But if I don't, just know that. You mean the world to me, and I'll do whatever it takes to protect you. I'll see you soon.

Love—yup, I'm gonna say it as much as I can from now on,

Mike

```
Date: 15 July 2010 12:34
From: John <Johnny5@yahoo.com>
To: Fred <fredwillow@earthlink.net>
CC: Terry Alexander
Subject: Save me a bullet
```

Uncle Fred,

I hope you get this; the damn zombies attacked at daybreak. They're inside killing everyone they see. I guess Sid was taking a cat-nap when they showed up. We've lost the old gymnasium. We thought we had them contained, man was that ever messed up thinking. They were on us before we knew it. These slow moving bastards surprised us. Damn hard to believe. I guess we got too cocky. The old gym looked like a good place to defend, limited entrances and high windows, now it's a death trap, they keep coming in and the only way out is past the rotten things.

I'm hiding in a janitor's closet with my lap top. I just hope the battery holds out for one more email. They haven't found me yet but believe me they will soon enough. They killed Bob and Agnes Farland on the front steps. They never had a chance to get inside.

Has to be a thousand of the damned things out there. They surrounded the building, and just waited for us to make a break for it, then they battered the doors down and swarmed in like a pack of slow moving locusts.

People were screaming all around me. A few people reached the weapons locker and tried to put up a struggle. I can hear gunfire outside the door, but it's all for nothing; there's just too many zombies. Mike Cooper's here; pass that tidbit on to Davey. He may still get a chance to put a bullet in Mike's brain. Bill and Martha Summers led the undead attack; at least we know what happened to them when they went out looking for food, poor bastards.

My fingers are shaking so badly, I'm having trouble finding the right keys—thank God for spell check. The screams are growing fainter, and now it's time for them to start munching. There's nothing quite like the sound of zombies devouring fresh intestines. The slurping, it's enough to drive a person insane.

I'm trying to stay focused, but it's almost impossible.

The place has suddenly gone quiet. The only sound is the shambling tread of these dead bastards. Why did this have to happen to us? Why did this have to happen to the world? What did we do to deserve this?

I know these questions will never be answered. Maybe they aren't meant to be answered. For all we know, this is how things were meant to be. Don't come back here, Uncle Fred, whatever you do, don't come back, this place is lost.

Try to make it to Fort Muskogee. Let them know what's going on and tell them to get ready for an attack. Stock up on food, water and ammunition, because it's liable to be a long battle. These things won't quit. They just keep coming and coming.

The shuffling is getting louder, they're at the door. Maybe I'll get lucky and they'll pass me by. I know it's unlikely. If I make it, I'll make my way north.

I wish I had a pistol. I'd end this quickly and eat a bullet. I don't want to be turned, to be one of them.

Do me a favor and take us out quick when the attack comes. You'll be seeing a lot of old friends, too. Remember, we're not what we used to be, and if we get through, save the last bullet for yourself.

My time is almost up; they're beating on the door. It won't be long now. First one through the door is in for a surprise, I'm gonna bust this lap top over its head. I plan to go out fighting.

You've always been there for me, Fred. I wish I could be there for you. You're like the father I never had. Remember, if you see me later and I'm changed, save a bullet for me.

Your nephew,

John

Date: 15 July 2010 14:25
From: Suzette <suzysmail@yahoo.com>
To: Sharon <Sharonmeller@medent.com>
CC: Tiara Chukwu
Subject: MOM READ THIS ASAP

Mom,
Hi how r u? I'm fine for now but there have been weird sounds coming from beyond the door outside and I'm scared.
I haven't slept since yesterday, all i can hear are the sounds of people screaming and those things howling from down the hallway.
How are you and Dad doing? I know Dad's bad leg is problly going to slow him down a bit, but I'm praying for u when i think about things.
I hope u can still get emails wherever you are. I'm sending this to your old email address because I'm not sure if you ever got a new one when we stopped using 'aol', so whatever; here goes. I probably won't have the chance to resend it if the email comes back to me.
Anyway, what happened today for me was i stopped by at my locker after class and noticed some girls in the bathroom across the hall making a lot of noise. Most of the kids at school had already gotten on the bus, but i forgot some stuff and missed it anyway. I heard the noises and thought they might be smoking in there (i no u told me to stop but seriously, I'm eighteen and its legal. so whatever. I can stop whenever i want later on if i live i guess). So i went in and found a bunch of girls rolling around on the floor, biting each other.
That was really weird, i mean nobody expects to find people rolling around and i thought they were making out (it's kind of popular right now, i guess? i dunno) but one of them actually took a piece out of the other girl's neck and there was blood on the floor.
i backed out quietly and tried to go find a teacher, but by then people were biting each other in the hallway, too. Julie from homeroom had Cassie from two lockers over from mine, pinned against the glass wall facing the courtyard, and was chewing on her face. i

heard the classroom doors locking as people hid themselves away and called the police, who i dunno, might be here right now or might not be. i can't really tell.

i ran into the library where I hid behind some shelves for a while until i thought it was okay to come out. There was a laptop on a table and I grabbed it and that's how I'm writing this email now because i think it might be safe to come out. Who knows, problly not, but whatever. i need to take the chance or whatever.

i read on the internet that there are more sick people in town walking around and nobody knows why. i hope you and Dad are safe and hiding someplace where you don't need to run too much. Please take care of Dad and if possible feed my fish.

            I love you Mom.

                Suzette

```
Date: 13 July 2010 16:46
From: Kyle <SuperNW@aol.com>
To: Dad <Ezvan65_g@bellsouth.com>
CC: Kyle Signoretti
Subject: Nothing left but home
```

Dad,

I fear this will be my final email to you. I don't even know if you received the other ones that I sent you. Who knows how long the power will stay on. I'm surprised it's lasted a whole week so far. I pray you're still alive. I hate not knowing.

I can hear the moans of the dead outside. They've started to gather in packs outside of the dorm. I believe they can smell our flesh in the air. At night, you can hear them scratching and banging on the doors, trying to get in. I'm glad we were able to barricade ourselves inside when the outbreak first began. There is still quite a few of us here. We're holding out hope that the army will come looking for survivors, but everything seems so bleak.

Yesterday, my girlfriend Emily was bit. She volunteered to go with a group to find food. I was too scared to go. When they returned, she had a bite on her hand. She got sick last night and died. About an hour later she was outside my door, trying to get in. I bashed her head in with a baseball bat. I guess the rumors were true. If you get bit, you turn into one of them. I'm still finding it hard to bare the guilt. I know it had to be done; I just wished it wasn't me that ended her life. Her blood is still stained on my clothes, and her moans of agony are still seared in my brain.

I'm starting to think there's nothing left for me here. I don't know if I can face this threat alone. Sure, there are other people here, but they all seem so distant from each other, and most seem to be as scared as I am, maybe even more so. I'm trying to decide if I should make my way to you. It so hard not knowing if your alive or not. I can't get the thought out of my mind. It's only a three hour drive back home to Boston and I could be there before nightfall. With a little luck, I could make it to my car, if it's not destroyed. Besides, I'm a lot faster than the undead that stalk the outside. They only seem to walk; I don't think they're capable of running. If I could just find some courage, I know I could make it.

Some of the dead outside are starting to get louder and more violent. I think they realize they're closer to finding their way in. I think it may just be a matter of time before they break through. I believe this helps with my decision. Do I wait here to be slaughtered like a lamb, or do I take the chance and fight for my survival, and make my way to you?

I'm going to go for it. There's no use just waiting to die here.

I'm coming home Dad...

```
Date: 14 July 2010 11:32
From: Tina Harper <Harper_family@live.com>
To: Joe&Maggie <Joeharper@gmail.com, Maggie34
harper@yahoo.com>
CC: Nelia Thompson
Subject: I love you both
```

Joseph and Maggie,
I wish I was there with you right now, but I can't get out of the building. I've been praying you've made it home from school safely, and are now together in the house. You should have enough food for a while. Fill the bathtubs with water, just in case the pipes should dry up.
The dead are returning to life. Real life zombies, as hard as it is to believe it.
Stay in the house, close all the doors and windows, and lock them. Don't let anyone in. I think there's some plywood in the basement, and maybe some nails. Try to cover as many of the first floor windows as possible.
I wish your father and I had stayed together, then I wouldn't have to work, and I'd be there to take care of you both. I'm sorry we failed to be the parents you needed, that you deserved. I love you two so much.
More than likely, I won't make it home. It seems impossible right now. I've looked out the window and down into the street, and there are hundreds, possibly thousands of zombies outside. We don't even know if there's any in the building. I'm betting there are. Apparently, they're too dumb to use the elevators, but I don't know how long that will last. After all, all one of them has to do is bump into the button on the wall, and then walk in.
Sorry, that's not important right now.
I love you. Please remember that. Always remember that. I'd give anything to be there right now. To be with you, and protect you from all of this. To shelter you from all the bad things and evil in this world. But that's not how things have worked out. I can only hope I've raised you to be responsible, and that I've given you the tools you'll need to survive.

I can hear people screaming out in the hallway. I need to go see what's going on.

I'll email you again in a bit of I can.

Love you,

Mom

```
Date: 14 July 2010 11:48
From: Tina Harper <Harper_family@live.com>
To: Joe & Maggie <Joeharper@gmail.com, Maggie34
harper@yahoo.com>
CC: Nelia Thompson
Subject: Be safe
```

What I feared has happened. A small group of zombies has made it to our floor. My boss, Roger, killed them. It took a little while, but he figured out if you hit them in the head, it'll kill them for good! Remember that, kids, hitting them in the head kills them. That will be key to your survival.

I'm sorry for any mistakes I've made as your mother. I'm sorry for anything I ever did to hurt you, or disappoint you.

I should have taken you for ice cream more often. I should have let you stay up late to watch that movie last week. I would give anything to have that time back, to say yes, and snuggle with you with a tub of popcorn on my lap. It shouldn't have mattered that I was too tired from work. I should have let sleep go, and held you.

I'm sorry we didn't have pizza more often, and insisted on cooking; taking more time away from you, just to save money.

I'm sorry we didn't get the swimming pool, and that I didn't send you to camp like you wanted. You should have gone. You should have had fun, instead of being stuck at home all summer with nothing to do. All that money I have in my savings account, for the future, seems so stupid now.

Forgive me for everything, please!

Roger needs help, he says he's sick, I'm going to go help him. I will write back if I can. I love you both so much.

Mom

```
Date: 14 July 2010 12:05
From: Tina Harper <Harper_family@live.com>
To: Joe & Maggie <Joeharper@gmail.com, Maggie34
harper@yahoo.com>
CC: Nelia Thompson
Subject: Goodbye
```

Roger was bitten and we didn't know it. He just turned into a zombie and bit my neck when I went to help him. I'm bleeding very badly and it won't stop. It's so hot as it squirts through my fingers. I love you both. Stay strong. Hold onto each other.
Don't ever forget that you were my world. I loved every moment of being your mother, and I'm very proud of you both.
My strength is going; I'm bleeding to death. Pretty soon I'll be one of them.
Take care of each other, please.
I love you with all my heart,
Mom

```
Date: 11 July 2010 12:44
From: Bob <BCcaster87@yahoo.com>
To: Mary <MarRobbin2@comcast.net>
CC: Anthony Giangregorio
Subject: One last thought
```

Dear Mary,
I don't know how much time I have but I had to email you this one time while I still can.

I... I don't even know how to begin. After all, from the first time I saw you I knew I loved you. Remember at the cafeteria when you dropped your purse? That was me who swooped in and picked it up for you.
I can only hope this email gets to you and doesn't end up in your spam file because this will be the last email I will ever send.
See, the living dead are about to break into my house and I know it won't be pleasant.
So I just wanted to tell you what I never had the courage to say to you in person.
Wait...I hear something coming from the back of the house. It's louder than the usual pounding of the dead I've heard before. I'll be right back.

Okay, so it was nothing. One of the zombies managed to knock a board off a window. I quickly nailed it back on and for the moment I'm safe. But not for long, I know. As more of them arrive, eventually there will be too many for me to stop them all together.
I'm sorry, I got off track, I do that sometimes. It's funny, I just keep typing my thoughts, not even realizing I'm doing it.
To get back on track...
I've wanted to talk to you ever since that first day but each time I tried, I would chicken out at the last second. No matter how many times I tried to get the courage up, something inside me would always stop me. I know, silly, isn't it? I mean, I will talk to hundreds of people by email every day, even flirt with a few of the women, and when it came down to actually talking to someone in person, I folded like a proverbial deck of cards.
And believe me, I wanted to so badly.
I think it was your hair I noticed first. Its auburn brown color, long, the way it caressed your shoulders. Then I followed down the curve of your shoulders to the small of your back. I admired the way your dress hugged you like a second skin. I have to admit though the love was already there, there was more than a little lust as well.
Huh, funny, I could never have said that to you in person. I don't know what it is about email, I find it so freeing.

Oh shit, there's another loud crash, I'll be right back...

Okay, three more tried to get in and this time one actually did. As the first one crawled through the kitchen window, a protruding nail caught its side, and hard as this is to believe, the nail began pulling on its skin like the ghoul was wearing a loose jumpsuit. As I watched in horror, the nail held fast and the skin began to stretch, to separate from the body until it finally tore free.
Underneath were the black and red muscles and tendons, making the zombie look like an anatomy experiment.
I had a rolling pin prepared for just such an occurrence, and though my eyes were closed, I used it on the ghoul's head like a bludgeon. I will never forget the meaty *thwack* as wood met skull but I do know the zombie went down.
I left the broken body where it lay, its brains seeping out of the large gash I made in its head. I tried to ignore the congealed blood spread across my kitchen floor, but I swear, I almost began to clean it up.
The other two weren't as persistent and I was able to push them back outside and board the windows up yet again.

So, where was I?
Oh yeah, I was trying to tell you something...something I've never had the courage to tell you until now.
So Mary, I know you basically don't even know me, I know that other than a few polite smiles in the hallway on the way to the copy machine, you've never so much as looked at me, but I just wanted to say that I lo....
Oh damn, they're in!
Oh my God, there's so many of them. They're coming through the windows, oh shit! They just knocked down the front door! They're coming in, swarming into my home. I know I shouldn't be typing still but there's no way I can fight them off and even if I did, what's the point?

The world is overrun by them. For all I know, you're not even alive any longer. For all I know, this email will go into your inbox and never be read, lost in the quagmire of the internet forever.

Uh, one of them has me....I...punched it.

I can't keep this up, Mary...

Ow, the bastard bit me!

I'm typing with one hand now, the other is bleeding so bad I think the damn zombie got an artery.

Ah, another has my leg. I...Mary, this is it, I'm sorry I never talked to you, I wish I had now.

Now that's it's over, I can't help but think of all the lost chances, all the times I could have done something, said something, but instead I hesitated, and my God I wish I could do it all over again.

Mary, if your still alive, be safe, and know that out there in the world, there is someone who loves you more than life itself.

Ow, dammit it, that one took off a piece of my thigh! Jesus all the blood!

Oh God, my neck, that one tore out my neck! Christ it's bleeding really bad, its spurting through my fingers. It's so warm and sticky, I never really knew just how warm blood can be...

I can't...see straight...getting woozy. Huh, it's funny, I don't even feel them eating me anymore...

If I become one of them, if you are one already, I promise that this time, if I see you in the new world—the dead world—somehow, someway, I will remember who I am, who you are, and...

This time...I will talk to you...

```
Date: 2 July 2010 07:16
From: Lyle <To0Cool4U@hotmail.com>
To: Marie <SecretsMarie@gmail.com>
CC: Lyle Perez-Tinics
Subject: Stay Home!
```

Honey,

I just tried calling you, but the phones aren't working. The internet is still up so I'm sending this email to warn you. Whatever you do, don't come into work today! You're probably still asleep, but when you get this turn the TV on. I'm sure this is already on the news.

It's happening! The dead are coming back to life, and they're eating people. I freaking told you it was going to happen someday. I don't have time to rub it in. They're far more disgusting than watching them in a movie. I saw one of the zombies walking around with no eyes. Goo or whatever started bubbling out of its eye sockets. I'm not telling you this to freak you out, but I'm just warning you to stay inside. Don't come into the city, they seem to be everywhere now, and I barely made it into the office. I didn't notice them when I left the house, you know the back roads, I never see anyone in the morning.

When I got into Temecula, I saw people running out of buildings, but I didn't see any of the dead at the time. When I pulled into the office parking lot, I saw a huge group of them just standing around. I thought they were waiting for me to turn the alarm off to the building. I walked up and they instantly noticed me. It was so disturbing because they all stared at me at the same time. They had this confused look on their pale faces. When I got closer to them, I noticed they looked dead, I mean really dead, but moving. They moved almost like robots. Remember the guy with no eyes? Well, another one was missing an arm and blood dripped out of its nub, and now that I was closer, I saw most of them had bloody wounds.

After I almost crapped my pants, I ran to the nearest door. I'm so glad I didn't forget my keycard in the car like I always do. After I got in, I turned off the alarm then set it again with me inside. The automatic door locks kick in when the alarm activates.

I started looking out the windows and its absolute chaos out there. The dead are shambling toward people, they're biting each other and there's a lot of blood pools with corpses lying next to pieces of bodies. Gunshots are ringing out every few seconds. I hope no one mistakes me for a zombie when I try to get out of here. The news websites are basically updating every few minutes. Nothing new, just the same 'the dead are walking and eating the living' spiel.

The dead know I'm in here so they keep banging on the door. From what I've seen, they're slow and smell really bad. The odor is seeping through the door cracks and I'm already gagging. I don't know how much longer the locks will hold. I hope you read this before you leave the house. I don't know how I'm going to get out of here.

I think maybe I'll break a window on the other side of the building and climb out that way.

Lyle

```
Date: 2 July 2010 07:49
From: Will <TooCool4U@hotmail.com>
To: Marie <SecretsMarie@gmail.com>
CC: Lyle Perez-Tinics
Subject: Stay Home!
```

They made it into the break room, and now I can hear them thrashing around and moaning. It sounds like there are hundreds of them in there. I gotta get out of here before I'm next for break-fast. This is my plan, I'm going to break the window that leads to the parking lot, jump out, get in my car, and get the hell out of here. Sounds like a good plan to me. My nerves are getting to me, and I'm having a hard time typing.

Just in case something happens, I want to tell you that I love you very much. You're the best thing to come into my life and I'll always thank you for that. Tell Kally I love her very much too. She's only two, so if you guys survive this, she might not remember me.

You know what's worse than knowing I might die out here? It's knowing I might not be able to see her grow up. Dammit, all of those things she does, you know, when she blows me kisses or says, "Hug daddy?" They're all flashing in my head. Tears are running down my face as I type this. God, I love you two so much. I hear them coming up the hallway. If I'm going to try to get out of here, it's now or never. I'll see you when I get home and don't worry about me. Remember all those zombie books I've reviewed over the years? I'm a zombie apocalypse pro. If anyone can handle this I can.

Love,
Will

Date: 11 July 2010 08:15
From: Tammy <TammySterling@gmail.com>
To: Rose <Rose_sterling@yahoo.com>
CC: Jessica A. Weiss
Subject: Mom

Dear Mom,
I've been trying to call for days now but have only been getting a busy signal. Today when I called there was nothing, just dead air. I hope you're all right.

Something isn't right around here. A week ago Henry was sent out of town because of a breakdown in the National Security Communications Network. I haven't heard from him in a week and I'm worried.

Normally I'd just assume he was really busy but he was sent out *your* way and I can't reach you either. Everyone I try to call on the west coast is unreachable—and I need some help. Even the news has been strangely lacking—which is a bad sign.

Yesterday, when he got home from school, our oldest son went to bed early and I still can't get him out of bed. The other kids are disinterested in everything, even eating.

To tell the truth, I'm not feeling quite myself either. If you get this, please call. I'm sorry for moving so far away from you and leaving you alone.

I love you.

Best in everything,

Tammy

```
Date: 12 July 2010 12:36
From: Tammy <TammySterling@gmail.com>
To: Bert <BertSterling@live.com>
CC: Jessica A. Weiss
Subject: Dad
```

Dear Dad,

Please receive this!

I know you haven't spoken to Mom since the divorce and you may not care, but I haven't heard from her, and though I just sent her an email yesterday, I wanted to contact you, too. My own husband is unreachable and the phone lines to you in Colorado won't connect.

My oldest son died this morning! He slept for two days and wouldn't wake up. When I tried to wake him today, his body rolled off the bed and he was oozing blood and yellow fluid from everywhere! And that was when I saw the bite on his leg. He had hidden it from me!

But it was when he stood up, looking sick, that I really freaked out. His brothers and sister came in to see him and he attacked them. He bit them! He bit me! Then I forced him off them and locked him in his room. I called the police.

We need help over here, Daddy. I'm scared. The rest of the children didn't even cry when the police took their brother's body, they just walked away and went to their rooms, after I told them to clean those bites. Now when I talk to them, they stare blankly at me.

I don't know what to do. Call me when you get this. I've been puking blood and the smell of cooked food makes it worse. I'm scared now that I have whatever he had. And the other children, he bit them, too!

Email me back as soon as you get this...please!

Your daughter,
Tammy

```
Date: 13 July 2010 07:13
From: Tammy <TammySterling@gmail.com>
To: Henry <sportsnut66_5@yahoo.com>
CC: Jessica A. Weiss
Subject: Where are you?
```

Dear Henry,

Where the hell are you? The children all died last night, and then believe it or not, they came back from the dead! I locked them in their rooms and called the police.

I haven't been out of the house since the police took the children. They had to gag and tie them up! And they wouldn't answer my questions or tell me where they were taking them. You should've been here! Damn your job! Damn security! You're needed at home!

I've been getting sicker and it's getting worse. The house is so quiet now I can hear the wind all day—it sounds like its alive and in pain.

It's unusually quiet outside, no animals roaming the woods or dogs barking, but I sometimes see some of our neighbors walking around. They look sick, too, and a few looked like they're bleeding. If you get this, come home, I don't know how much longer I have. My eyes are blood shot and my skin is an odd shade of yellow. My gums are bleeding and my teeth are loose. Something is really wrong.

Just come home, I love you.

Your wife,

Tammy

Date: 12 July 2010 08:51
From: Tammy <TammySterling@gmail.com>
To: <cbty@live.com, caddilacman1959@inlook.com, c2gu_barbtroy1968@gmail.com, callsend@zsn.net, candyred32@smail.com, dogladyh7@zmail.com, chipsahoy54@zsn.net, brokenroddg54@yahoo.com>
CC: Jessica A. Weiss
Subject: Anyone

To Anyone Who Gets This,

I'm sending this to everyone in my address book though I doubt I'll be around to read any replies.

I can't reach my family in California or Colorado. My husband left for California over a week ago and I haven't heard from him either. All of my children and neighbors have died and have returned from the dead. I've been getting sicker and sicker, too. I'm alone in South Carolina and scared and I know it's my turn to die now.

Before the TV went out, they were talking about the end of the world, that the dead were walking everywhere.

I swear I can hear my children outside calling for me to come to them every night—but I refuse to open the curtains, not since I watched a rotting man lunge at my front door. Sometimes I even hear footsteps on the porch and faint scratching at the door. But that isn't possible, is it?

I'm starting to think I'm the only one still alive anymore. Twitter and Facebook are having 'server errors' and I can't access anything or anyone. This feels like the end of the world—but also a new beginning of something else.

So to anyone still out there: PLEASE HELP ME.

After I send this email, I think I'll close my eyes for a while, I'm so very tired.

I have a feeling I won't wake up again, well, at least not the same.

Tammy

Date: 16 July 2010 14:39
From: Julie <lolipop8790@hotmail.com>
To: Margie <margiethecook@earhtlink.com>
CC: Carrie Cuinn
Subject: Hi Mom

Dear Mom,
This isn't a joke, this is very serious, so please pay attention and read all the way through. Right now I'm so glad that you live out in the middle of nowhere and I'm sorry, you're right, I should never have moved into the city.

It wasn't the crime, like you were worried about, or living in a bad neighborhood. It was the zombies. We've had an outbreak and now they're out there, they're just outside my apartment and I'm not ever going to get to see you to tell you in person how much I missed you after I moved.

They got Kevin a few minutes ago. I know you've been angry with him for the last few years, since you thought he took me away from you, but he was the best husband. He died saving me, or at least getting me into the apartment so I'd have a chance. I don't think anyone is coming to save me now, but Kevin stood between me and those things so I could fumble with the keys, and they bit him to death while he shoved me through the door. I keep thinking I took too long, that I killed him because I couldn't get the damn front door open in time.

We were walking home from coffee at that cute little place down the block, the one I keep saying I'll take you to if you ever come visit, but you don't want to leave the dogs alone all weekend so you've never come. You never saw where we lived, never sat on my couch and watch the sun come in through the old stained glass windows that turned this place from being a tiny studio walk-up into something magical. I love my life here, and all I wanted to do was share it with you.

I'm in the closet in the bedroom with my laptop and I hear them out there. I don't think I have a lot longer and if they come for me I'm going to hit send wherever I am in the email because you need to see this. The government is saying it's a crime wave because of how hot it's been this summer. The newspaper said it's homeless people having some kind of uprising, but that's not true. What a horrible lie. They could have saved us if they had just told us what was really going on. I'm not going to let that happen to you. Don't waste time trying to call me or the police, just board up your windows and keep the dogs inside.

I know you've got Dad's old service pistol in the box on the top shelf of your closet. The one you didn't want me to know about, but kids snoop around, okay? I'm sorry I looked, because you told me not to, but I'm glad I did because now I know you've got that to protect you. Put the bullets in it, and if you need to use it, hold the gun in both hands.

Oh God!

They're in the apartment now and I know they'll hear me typing but I don't care, I have to tell you that I love you and I always have, even when we didn't talk, even when I snuck out that night and ran off to marry Kevin and we should have invited you. I told myself you wouldn't have come anyway but I wanted you there.

I cried for an hour afterwards, because it didn't feel right without you and I know you think I didn't care about you, but oh God, please check your email Mom. I hear them. I love you and please make sure you...

```
Date: 1 July 2010 10:00
From: Robert Christian < robchris-
tian419@zmail.com>
To: <callects@zsn.net, caddyman1959@inlook.com,
candrew89@zmail.com, catladyx6@zmail.com,
c2gu_barbara1968@zmail.com, chipsh0t@zsn.net,
calebroxxx69@zmail.com, cUl8@inlook.com>
CC: Dan Larnerd
Subject: Spam of the Dead

Mister Robert Christian
Greatest National PLC
Leeth Road Branch
London

Dearest Friend,
I am Robert Christian, a barrister and Accounts
Manager at the Greatest National PLC, Leeth Road
```

Branch. I hope you and your family are well in this time of international crisis. By God's blessing, I have a very important opportunity for you! We found your name in your national directory, and since you are of high character, we chose you specifically.

As you know, the undead have began to walk the streets and devour the living. This is very sad. I hope this has not happened to you. It just so happens that our beloved Prince of Nigeria was killed by these horrible monsters. Our brave Prince was fleeing the capital when the royal limousine was overrun. When hearing that her husband and his mistress were torn to pieces, his wife shot herself. The Prince had two heirs but one was also killed by the undead and the other fell from a helicopter. Now the barricades in Nigeria have fallen and the dead rule the streets. Surely, you have seen this?

From past experience, I know that no one else will come forward to claim the prince's fortune. This, by God's blessing, is where we need your help. As the Fund's Manager was eaten alive while stuck in a revolving door, I am able to transfer the prince's vast fortune to you.I, in conjunction with a surviving colleague (the Chief Operating Officer at the bank), now seek your permission to do so. We are writing you because of the emergency restrictions put in place by the government in this time of crisis do not allow us to operate with so much money.

Here are my instructions to you. I would like you to immediately send us your FULL NAME, ADDRESS, PHONE NUMBER, BANK ACCOUNT NUMBERS and BANK STATUS (operating, looted, overrun) that we may begin this transaction. The money will be released into your account at a ratio of 70% to our 30%. There is no risk AT ALL and we shall do all the necessary paperwork so you may concentrate on defending your family.

By God's blessing, we hope you act swiftly on this opportunity.

Do not think your money would be better invested in ammunition, for when this crisis is over, you will regret it very much.
Thanks and Regards,

Robert Christian

Date: 10 July 2010 08:24
From: Mike <jconners@comst-umi.com>
To: Susan <darling33@top.com>
CC: Rebecca Besser
Subject: A different war

My love,
This morning the base was attacked. Not by the enemy, at least not the one we're here to fight, but by something else. Zombies. I know that sounds crazy, and hell, maybe I am going crazy.
But a group of walking, rotting corpses came stumbling into our command center and started attacking people. The woman that was working next to me had her throat ripped out. Some rotting man just bit into her and started eating. Blood was shooting out of her wounds, all over the place; on the equipment, on the walls of the tent, on everyone within ten feet!
We were quick to act, but not quick enough to save her. Sergeant Milton pulled his sidearm and fired two rounds into the ghoul's head, stopping it from feasting further.
As he turned to leave Command to find out what was going on outside, two more entered and attacked him. He didn't even have time to raise his weapon to fire again. I knew what I needed to do. I pulled one of the zombies off Sergeant Milton and pressed the

barrel of my sidearm to its forehead. I pulled the trigger and its brains splattered to the sand-covered ground with a splat. The other zombie, the one that violently dispatched Sergeant Milton, bit my arm before I could turn away.

I blew that ghoul to hell, too. He didn't even see it coming.

Together, those of us that were still able, fought off the remaining undead. But it didn't last long, as those that had been killed started to reanimate and attempted to kill us.

We fought as long as we could, but had to retreat. We're now in the middle of the desert, in a Humvee, hoping to find somewhere safe for the night. We're behind enemy lines. Afghanistan is a dangerous place without the added worry of being eaten alive by walking corpses that have come back from the dead.

Those of us that were wounded have fevers and are vomiting blood. Our fear is we will become like our attackers; mindless walkers, seeking flesh. I fear that soon, I'll be dead, at least dead to my humanity.

I don't know even if this email will make it to you, as my satellite uplink is buggy, and the signal comes and goes. But if you do receive this, know that I love you and am thinking of you. Damn, I lost the signal completely, and I'll have to send this later.

Hopefully before it's too late.


```
Date: 10 July 2010 08:25
From: Mike <jconners@comst-umi.com>
To: Susan <darling33@top.com>
CC: Rebecca Besser
Subject: I miss you
```


I've been lying in the sand, trying to get some sleep, thinking of home, and I knew I had to let you know what was on my mind. I keep thinking about the way your hair smells, and the way you look in the morning, waking up beside me, smiling at me softly. Your sleepy blue eyes fluttering open and then shut again.

I remember the way your lips taste when I kiss you. Your lips are so soft; after our first kiss I couldn't get enough of you.

When I close my eyes, and my fever runs high, I swear I can feel your soft body beside me, and I want you. I know it's delirium, but it's real to me for that moment. I'll miss you, my precious love. But even though the thought of leaving you devastates my heart, the thought of our daughter hurts me more. I'll never get to hold her precious newborn body in my arms and cuddle her close. I'll never get to kiss her forehead or her cheeks. I won't be there when she says her first word or takes her first step. I won't be there when she falls in love or goes on her first date. I won't be there to be her father, which I deeply regret.

Will you tell her about me? About how much I love her and wish I was there for all the things she'll experience in life? Will you kiss her for me?

Oh, God, I hurt all over, and my hands are shaking. Death is coming and there's nothing I can do to stop it.

Protect her, keep her safe. If this thing spreads stateside, you'll have to take care of her, because I won't be there. Stock up on food, water, and ammo. Keep the handgun–the one I gave you for protection–close at hand and loaded. Shoot to kill. Shoot them in the head. God, I hope this doesn't happen there. I hope it hasn't happened already and you're still alive to read this.

It's getting harder and harder to breathe, and the wound on my arm is throbbing and on fire. I have to go… I don't want to. I want to come home to you and be your husband. I want to be a father to our daughter. I can't do either. So, I'm sending my love with this email, praying that God will align the satellites and get this to you in time to save you. Wait, there it is, the satellites working! I'm gonna send you both emails at the same time.

I love you, babe. You were the highlight of my life. Protect our little girl, love her with all the love you have for me, because she's the only part of me you'll have left.

Love you for eternity,

John

```
Date: 12 July 2010 11:20
From: Lorrie <Girlpwer@mendent.com>
To: David <watr99_4@live.com >
CC: Barb Signoretti
Subject: Farewell my love
```

My dearest David,

As I write this to you to, I hope you're safe. I know Iraq isn't a safe place right now, but it's safer than being home here at the base. Don't worry about us; we'll be in a better place by the time you read this.

As you know, today was Patti Savard's eleventh birthday party next door. I decided to take a nap, but I was soon wakened by delirious screaming from outside. I opened the front door to witness by what I can only describe as sheer chaos. People were screaming and running…blood was everywhere! I thought we were being attacked by terrorists, but it was people we know—our friends and neighbors! It makes no sense, they seem to be alive, but with wild, dead, empty eyes.

People are running…biting…slaughtering…eating everyone—its madness! Steve Faulk is dead. Mallory Lynde was hovering over him like an animal and was chewing on—what looked like—his liver! Little Tommy Thornton caught up with Father Lisbon and knocked him on his back—his head hit a rock—it sounded like Gallagher had smashed a watermelon. Tommy then pounced and starting gnawing the father's groin…knowing you, you can find a joke in there somewhere! Don't take me wrong, I'm not making light of the situation—it's so horrifying. I'm so scared. I feel like I'm losing my mind, but I want you to know what's happening. I think my subconscious is starting to take over…maybe a defense mechanism to keep me from going into shock.

I looked back to the Savard's house to try to find the kids. That's when I saw Colonel Savard come out of his house with a gun. Patti, in her blood-soaked party dress, was running toward him with that crazed look—and he shot her!

She stumbled but didn't fall, and she jumped on him, knocked him over and landed on his chest, then started biting his neck. She's only eleven, how did she get the strength to do that?

He got his arm free and shot her in the head!

She collapsed. Her brains were all over him! He got up and started shooting everyone! It's becoming hard to breathe, and I'm getting a bit dizzy.

Others who haven't been infected joined him, but don't worry, I was able to get Kyle and Kayla away before they shot them. It's like a war out there! Ironic isn't it? The kids were bit, but I was able to grab them and tie them up before they were strong enough to stop me.

They're in the basement. Kyle bit me while I was constraining him. It was just a little nip, but I'm afraid it's too late. I feel very cold and am getting numb. I think I can feel the 'infection' climbing up my spinal cord toward my brain. It feels weird.

Thank you for leaving the gun…you know, the one you said was 'just for emergencies'? I know what I need to do. I'll put the children out of their misery, and then I'll do the same for myself—before I lose my sanity completely.

We love you and are proud of you, hopefully you'll find it in your heart to forgive me for what I'm about to do.

With all my love,

Lorrie

```
Date: 2 July 2010 22:47
From: Katy <katywagner14@earthlink.net>
To: Michael <mikewagner12@live.com>
CC: Dane T. Hatchell
Subject: Bad news
```

Michael,

I can hardly bring myself to write this. So much has happened so fast. I wish you were here, I need you so bad. This is the third time now I'm attempting to send this email. I finally have enough bars on my phone that I feel it should make it.

We had to leave Chalmette. Things just went from bad to worse. I don't know what you know about the situation over here. God knows we don't know what's happening where you are in Afghanistan.

The story hit the news that the dead first began clawing out of their graves on April first. April first! Isn't that ironic? Fucking April fool's day! I was half asleep when I watched the news that night. It reminded me about last year's fake story where Taco Bell bought advertisement rights to the Liberty Bell and was renaming it the Taco Liberty Bell.

But the living dead story was still on the next day. I didn't understand how this could be real. I still don't.

And now, three months later, the you-know-what has hit the fan All of this is madness, I'm so depressed. There's so much you need to know. I don't know how to tell you. Please, brace yourself.

Kenny and Marsha brought their kids over to your mom and dad's, so we could deal with this thing together. Your mom went hysterical at the news. It was worse when she saw Mrs. May on the television news. She and Mrs. May had been friends since they were in high school. She had been dead for just three weeks and Mom recognized her immediately. As if seeing her wasn't bad enough, her head exploded from a shotgun blast right there on the TV. Your mom fainted when she saw that. But it got worse, she may have had a mini-stroke. It happened so fast we didn't have time to take her to a doctor.

I tell you this because your mom did have a heart attack, or a stroke. She passed away. I'm sorry.

It happened during the night. We were all packed up, and ready to leave at the first light of the morning, when the dead broke into the house. It was more terrifying than you can imagine.

Kenny and your dad were well armed. I never knew your brother was that good of a shot. You can only kill those bastards by shooting them in the head. And sometimes you have to shoot them twice.

It was early in the first attack that your mother gasped and collapsed to the floor. I tried to give her CPR, but she had no pulse, and never took another breath. Your dad didn't even get to tell her goodbye, he was too busy protecting us.

Another gang of ghouls came before sunup, and we survived that. But just as we loaded up the van, and Kenny and your dad were loading your mom in the back, one of them snuck up on your dad and bit him on the arm. Kenny killed it with his pistol.

The bite didn't look too bad. We put alcohol on it and bandaged it. But not more than an hour later he started to go into convulsions. We stopped on the side of the highway and laid him on a blanket. His body shuddered and he went still and we thought he died, but then his eyes snapped open and he went completely crazy. His eyes were blood red and he snarled like a wild beast. He wouldn't stay away from us. Kenny was forced to shoot him.

It was horrible. It doesn't seem real when I put it into words. The children saw it all, and I don't like to think what it'll do to them, their psyche.

Barksdale Air Force Base is a hundred miles from where we are now. We're going to try and make it there. Kenny figures it's our best chance.

I agree.

I don't know how to do this. I've been avoiding it but you must know. Michael Jr. was asleep in your old bedroom during the first attack. They broke in through the window and entered the house that way. I was in the kitchen with the other adults.

I feel like it was my fault, I should have been there. He was so sweet, so innocent. He didn't deserve what happened to him. There was almost nothing left of his body by the time we got to him. I can only hope and pray he went quickly. I can't bear to think of our little baby suffering.

Don't hate me, I love you. I wish you were here with me. I miss my husband. I need you.

Katy

Date: 15 July 2010 10:24
From: <redsoxfan1963@netcast.com>
To: <rbdonaldson@comcast.com, samrobson@yahoo.com,
      pubcrawler69@britmail.co.uk, valley-
gal83@hotmail.com,sookyoungchoe@hyndai.com,
jamelake@dubaibank.com,msgtcbrown@gmail.com,
mariapesci@comcast.net, jane_dn_under@sydnaynet.com,
kiera2006@comcast.com, rebeccadowning@live.com,
cubsfan4ever@hotmail.com,
CC: Scott M. Baker
Subject: Is anyone out there?

I'm writing this quick. Don't know how much time I have. The power came back on about ten minutes ago. Been off for ten days. I don't know when it'll go out again.

The outbreak hit Boston two weeks ago. When it started to go to shit, I wanted to head north while we still could get out of the city and hide out in Maine until it blew over. Jill refused, insisting she was needed at the hospital. She called me two nights later, crying. The hospital was being overrun with zombies. She begged me to come get her. By then martial law was declared, and I couldn't leave the apartment without being detained or shot. It was the last I heard from Jill.

News reported this shit happening all over the world. Cable covered it live, at least until the government took over and started broadcasting nothing but press briefings that were all bullshit. Local news picked up the slack for another day or two before their reporters were killed. By then I didn't need TV–I watched the end of the world from my window.

The police and army abandoned us. Not that I blame them. Anyone who stayed behind was butchered. My neighbor and her kids tried to escape about a week ago; they made it as far as the parking lot before they were attacked by a few dozen of these things. They tried to get back inside but didn't make it. Now there's zombies roaming around on the first floor, so I can't get out even if I wanted to.

I've been raiding the neighbors' apartments for food and water. It's safe because the dead can't climb stairs. I have enough to last a few more weeks, but that doesn't matter. I'm not getting out of this alive.

I hope some of you made it. Let me know soon before I lose power again. God help us all.

<SEND>

```
Delivery notification failure: rbdonaldson@comcast.com
Delivery notification failure: samrobson@yahoo.com
Delivery notification failure: pubcrawler69@britmail.co.uk
Delivery notification failure: valleygal83@hotmail.com
Delivery notification failure: sookyoungchoe@hyndai.com
Delivery notification failure: jameblake@dubaibank.com
Delivery notification failure: msgtcbrown@gmail.com
Delivery notification failure: mariapesci@comcast.net
Delivery notification failure: jane_dnhunder@sydnaynet.com
Delivery notification failure: kiera2006@comcast.com
Delivery notification failure: rebeccadowning@live.com
Delivery notification failure: cubsfan4ever@hotmail.com
```

```
Date: 22 July 2010 13:12
From: Walter <WalterThomason@medent.com>
To: Lisa <LisaJordan@gmail.com>
CC: Grady Yandall
Subject: I'll see you soon
```

Hi Sunshine,

This will be my last email unless we make it out of here alive. I guess there are some things left to be thankful for in spite of this craziness. Satellite internet connections and a good supply of shotgun shells are at the top of the list. I picked the wrong time to go on a road trip through the bayou and now I'm stuck on the outskirts of New Orleans with some survivalists that are nearly as scary looking as the zombies trying to kill us. Still, I need to be thankful for these guys, too. They look like extras from that old movie Deliverance, but they're smart, strong and well armed. If they hadn't fought their way to my SUV after I hit a tree, I'd be dead now. Ben, Tommy, Red and Sam are the only men left alive besides me. Now we're holed up in what's left of their camp with some women and children. We've done our best to keep the monsters out of the main cabin, but it's a losing fight. They're knocking down the door as I type.

I've been watching online news reports about necromancers, voodoo witchcraft and zombies. The old hag they call 'Oracle' is claiming responsibility for this madness. She has a website now and her army of the undead is over running New Orleans. The latest reports say it all started after the new white mayor pissed her off by not letting her float into the Mardi Gras parade. She believed he was discriminating against her and decided to punish all the white people by unleashing zombies on them. Yeesh! So does that make these things racists since they only kill white people? It doesn't matter from where I'm standing.

But for every crackpot like her, there are others who say it's their fault. I don't know what to believe any more. Some of the guys think it's Judgment Day, others think it was a biological spill or radiation from space. Hey, it takes all kinds, right?

I have to go help with the fortifications, but I'll write back as soon as I'm done, I promise.

Love you,

Walter

```
Date: 22 July 2010 14:43
From: Walter <WalterThomason@medent.com>
To: Lisa <LisaJordan@gmail.com>
CC: Grady Yandall
Subject: I'll see you soon
```

Hi, sunshine.

As well prepared as these guys are, the zombies are hard to kill and they've taken over most of the compound. We have to evacuate and make for Texas. It seems like the Texans are making a good stand along their border. We've been in touch with some survivalists by a Satellite phone one of the guys has and they plan to meet us halfway.

I'm so sick of this. It's getting dark. Everyone here is ready to make a run for it. We're going to lure as many of the zombies into the cabin downstairs as we can and burn it down before we head west. We'll climb out the window and monkey our way through the trees to the caves where our trucks are parked. We made sure they were secure before using spare cans of gas to douse the buildings around us. The smell of gasoline is overpowering. We've left the natural gas lines open in the other buildings we could get to so that this whole place will go up like a roman candle. After we load up the vehicles and get far enough away, Ben will use his grenade launcher to ignite the cabin and send these things back to the Hell that spawned them. I volunteered to man the machine gun turret on the lead vehicle. My time with the Army Rangers in Iraq and Afghanistan is paying off. I've earned these guys' respect and they trust me.

I wish I had some kind of web-cam so we could talk one more time face to face before I head out, but paying an extra hundred dollars at the time wasn't an option we could afford. I want to let you know I'm sorry for the way I've acted since you asked me to leave. Splitting up was hard on me. I worked so hard to make you happy and when you said it wasn't enough, it broke my heart. I said a lot of mean things over the last few months and I'm... well, I'm sorry. Especially about fighting with you before coming out here. It seems so stupid now, like most of the things we get upset about. If Carrie wants to get a navel ring then tell her I said to go for it. She's sixteen and there are times when I'm too strict. We've laid a good foundation for her and she's our girl, so she'll be fine. Don't worry about me. Tell Carrie I love her and know I still love you, too. The zombies are piling into the cabin and I have to sign off. We left some fresh dead bodies downstairs as bait and they're too busy feasting on our dead brothers in arms to notice the smell of gas, that is if they can smell anything at all besides blood. I'll be back in town soon, but remember, aim for the head if I'm not breathing.

I'll see you soon, Lisa, I love you,
Walter

```
Date: 19 July 2010 20:23
From: Mark<megaMark@aol.com>
To: <Gummiebear92@fastmail.com>
CC: Tomara Armstrong
Subject: Come get me, please!
```

Dear Gummiebear92,

I just received your email, so surely you're sitting by your computer waiting for my reply. I appreciate your concern for me.

I have mass emailed my entire contact list in search of a quick reply, but I fear they're all dead. G-bear, you are my only hope.

The streets are crowded with walking dead people. They're moaning so loud… I can't stand it.

This town has gone crazy. The dead are running around eating everything that moves… the smell is unbelievable, and the battery in my lap top is almost dead. I'm on the roof of the public library at the corner of Broadway and Adams in Elk City, Oklahoma. Yes, I'm stealing their WiFi, but that doesn't mean I'm a bad person, Gummie.

Oh God… Mrs. Highsmith, who owns the antique shop across the street, just tried to shoo a couple of the undead off her doorstep with a broom. One grabbed her from behind and the other bit the nose right off her wrinkled face; she's bleeding all over the street and screaming.

Would you happen to have a helicopter? I know that's a stupid question, but I'm desperate. You could probably afford your own private jet from what I've heard about you. So, can you come save me? If so, that would be awesome!

Oh man, Mrs. Highsmith is laying face down on the road, and people just keep walking all over her. They're all over the library lawn; squishing their bodies up against the building like they want to lift it up and carry it somewhere.

I'll give you whatever you want. My parents have a couple of cars and a boat. It's all yours. Hell, you can even have the house, if you want it.

I think you would really like me, if we met. I'm 19, 5'11 with sandy blonde hair, and freckles. Do you like freckles? I do. I assume you're a girl, by the name, but if you're a guy, that's okay, too. Just say you'll come and get me, G-bear. Please, I'm begging you. Just say you can come and get me.

I'm going to send this email now, and hope you'll reply soon. I hope that whatever connection we've made will be strong enough to get us through this…to bring us together. Because I think we belong together, G-Bear. You and me…forever.

Elk City is a small town in western Oklahoma, but here are the GPS coordinate: 35.4119944, -99.4042592

Xoxo Mark

```
Date: 14 July 2010 14:37
From: Glenda <Glenda_Perkins@yahoo.com>
To: Emily <Emily_Diaze@fastmail.com>
CC: K.M. Rockwood
Subject: See you soon!
```

My dearest Emily,
You never expected to hear from me again, did you? I'm certainly not supposed to know your personal email address. A big celebrity like you, with layers of agents, personal assistants, bodyguards keeping the likes of me

from getting in contact with you. Yes, I remember those bodyguards well.

But I do know it! I always have. You'd be surprised what I know about you. I know where you are now, in a luxury resort on Changuu Island off the coast of Zanzibar. Secluded, unreachable and, temporarily, safe.

Did you know that Changuu is also called 'Prison Island'? It's where uncooperative slaves were once held. Coincidence? I don't think so!

I've never emailed you before. Little matter of restraining orders. And I knew as soon as I tried to contact you, the address would be changed.

Now what would be the point of changing it, even if it were possible? The zombies have made so many things undoable. I'm pleasantly surprised that the internet is still functioning. At some point, it will undoubtedly cease. Many cell phones no longer work and land lines have not operated for days.

Do you know where I've been since the trial? Do you care? Perhaps not. In the courtroom, you never looked at me. Not even as you told how frightened you were, how the movie studio had to put on extra security.

You were terrified I was going to show up in your bedroom again. I treasure the look on your gorgeous face as I made you remove your negligee. I would have shown you then and there what I had planned for us. If only we hadn't been interrupted!

After the conviction, I was held for further psychiatric evaluation and possible treatment. But legally, I'm sane. Obsessed, perhaps, but sane. The doctors say so, the judge says so. I was transferred to prison, and I've been here for over five years now.

In some ways being confined has been difficult. Do you remember that for years I was a merchant marine? So the cramped quarters don't bother me much. But to stay in one place for years, and to have no chance at all to catch a glimpse of you—that's hard.

Good jobs are hard to come by in prison, but I eventually managed to get a work assignment in receiving. My boss Glenda, a nasty old bitch who worked for the state for years, sat on her ass and read magazines while I did the work, unpacking and sorting incoming inventory. Magazines like 'People.' She let me have them when she was done with them—why not? What harm could I do, reading magazines? I saved every article that had your name or picture. That's a lot of articles.

And you know what? There's a computer in receiving, one with internet access. Computers with internet access are off limits to inmates. But if I didn't use the computer, Glenda would have had to do some work. As long as I was careful, I had access to the internet. Another way to track your activities. I'm even using her email account!

I doubt Glenda will be back. Not too many survivors out there, far as I can tell. No one shows up for work any-more—no guards, no kitchen staff, no counselors. So it's just us inmates here. Most of the poor souls are locked in their cells. They'll starve to death. Is that better or worse than being eaten by a zombie? I don't know. But those of us with no disciplinary problems were in dormitory-type housing and just had to force a few windows to escape. Most of them left the prison, probably to be eaten. A few of us smarter ones stayed until we could make some plans.

Barriers designed to keep prisoners from escaping are equally effective at keeping zombies out. I climbed one of the guard towers to take a look and saw that the outer perimeter—the three rows of razor wire—is full of zombies caught in it. They struggle, and don't care if body parts are ripped off, but some of them are so entangled they'll never get loose. If one of them does make it through the razor wire, it comes up against the stone wall and turns around, back to be caught up again.

In the tower, I found shotguns, flashlights and binoculars. There's a massive supply of food, clothing and blankets, etc. We'll be fine until the power goes out. Even then, there are emergency generators. At least until the fuel runs out.

But I digress. I'm making plans, my dearest Emily. For us. I know you don't think it now, but we belong together. We will be together.

Some of us broke into Riot Control Central, so we have riot gear, tear gas and a fine array of weapons. I don't know if tear gas will work against zombies, but it will work against people if we need it.

We're fortifying a heavy dump truck and loading it with supplies. We've attached the snow plow, which should work just fine for clearing zombies out of our path. Tomorrow we'll crash it through the west gates.

Then on to the Baltimore seaport where we'll assess available boats. Much depends on how much fuel we find. I would prefer a ship, but we can make do with a large sailing yacht.

I'll be captain! No one else knows how to sail or navigate, so everyone is dependent upon me. They will have to do as I say.

Our plan is to sail to a warm island surrounded by strong currents that will sweep away any zombies who try to approach Changuu Island.

I've told everyone it's in the Indian Ocean. They think that's near the Bahamas, and I see no reason to disabuse them of the idea. What does it matter? They have no idea how long it should take to get there anyway. When we finally get there with our arsenal, we'll have no trouble overrunning the island.

Then we will finally be together, you and I. You will have to obey me and honor my wishes, for it will be *me* who is caring for you and protecting you. I'm emailing you to give you time to get accustomed to the idea. I'll use force if I have to, but I hope you come to your senses and accept that, inevitably, you will be mine.

Until we meet again, my dearest,

Stanley

```
Date: 13 July 2010 09:42
From: Joshua <Joshbatter32@comcast.net>
To: Jarrod <JaarrodTT@bellsouth.net>
CC: Tony Schaab
Subject: The last (one-night) stand
```

Jarrod,

Dude, I had to write you and tell you what's going on. It's something so amazing, so mind-bogglingly inconceivable, that I'm not even sure I believe it's happened. It has literally turned my world upside-down.

I had SEX last night with Stacey, the hot R.A. from the girl's dorm across the street!

I know, its crazy, right? But after we left the bar last night, I was walking back to the dorm and saw her sitting outside on the benches in front of the building. I still can't believe they shut the bar down early, just because all those news reports of random violence had everybody scared...I mean it sucks that people are out there messin' around with other people, but a guy's gotta get his drink on, y'know? Especially in a college town like this, I mean really!

Anyway. So she was outside on the bench, and she was crying, right? She's all alone, and I guess the few beers we had at the bar earlier gave me some extra courage, so I went over to her and said hey. Thank God she remembered me from our Intro to Communications class last semester, or else I would have felt really dumb! We start talking, I asked her what's wrong, and she tells me she just broke up with her boyfriend—hello rebound! At least, I think she broke up with her boyfriend...she said they had a big fight or something, like he went crazy on her, hit her or something... some guys just don't know to appreciate what they have, I guess. He got her pretty good, she had a big bandage on her upper arm, but she seemed like she didn't want to talk about it too much, so I didn't press the issue.

I was feeling pretty good at this point, she'd stopped crying and I had made a few stupid jokes and got her to laugh a couple of times, so I pressed my luck and asked her if she wanted to come to my room and watch a movie or something. I thought for sure she'd give me one of those 'I can't tonight' excuses, but hot damn she actually said yes! She said she didn't want to be alone, which was freakin' awesome for me. So we went upstairs and I did the 'classic' move.

I put in a horror movie, so she might get scared and want to snuggle up to yours truly! I know, it's so eighth grade, but let me tell you, it worked like a charm. I put in that new movie I just got, the one where all the people go crazy and start killing each other, and before long she was in my lap. So we're still watching the movie, sorta, but one thing was leading to another, if you know what I mean...I don't even think we made it to the end of the flick before we moved to the bed!

Obviously I'm not gonna give you any more details about last night, you sick puppy, but I had to write you a quick note and let you know what went down last night. She's still sleeping in the bed in the other room. She didn't look too great when I got up, she's kinda pale in the face and her skin's kinda got this ashy color to it...those aren't signs of VD or anything, is it? I hope not.

I still can't believe it, dude. God, she's so hot, I could just die.

Shit, I just heard a crash from the other room...she must be up, I hope she's okay.

I wonder if sdddffffjjkkkkllljfffeeeddddd......

<<AUTO-SEND>>

```
Date: 22 July 2010 20:32
From: Ian <IanPBellamn54@smail.com>
To: Devan <DD_Bellman2@hotmail.com>
CC: E. F. Schraeder
Subject: Get upstate!
```

Devan

This is it, bro. I don't think you'll hear from me again today. I've been hammering boards across the windows all day trying to block those freakin' monsters from getting into Mom and Dad's house. They're gone, you probably figured. They got attacked this morning on their way to work. Mom and Dad were going to work assuming, like usual, that it wasn't happening here.

I think they got to Kessler Street at the end of the neighborhood. One cell call was all I got, then the line went dead. I can only figure they're zombified now, clawing out someone else's eyes, ripping apart skin. Mom always liked to tear into us, but I'm hoping like hell she doesn't get the chance to do it literally. Okay, I guess that's not funny. I must be in shock to be joking right now. Man, you're so lucky you can't hear what I'm hearing; the sound of screams and groans, breaking bones, smashing glass. Nothing else can drown it out, no matter how loud I play music or anything. You name it and it's going on outside. Our neighbor's house didn't stand a chance.

The undead horde came charging through real early, tearing up everything that stood in their way, ripping down road signs, breaking through doors and windows, pulling people out of showers and beds and just gnawing into them while they screamed. Oh man, it was hideous. I hope it's better where you are. I never saw such a bloody mess in my life.

I figure we're lucky we grew up in a brick house, that's one more layer of resistance we have in this crazy war against the undead. I brought little Jessica from next door over when I saw her pawing at her garage door, trying to get away from a herd of zombies chasing her down the street. They were mauling everything they saw, people included. David Radcliff from your school got grabbed from behind, and a sickly mass of squirming bodies pulled him down onto the grass. You could hear him screaming while they were shredding him and snapping him apart like a candy bar. When the pile stopped gnawing, finally, and started to crawl their way toward Jessica, there was nothing much left of David. Jessica just kept pounding on the door for help, but there was no one there, so I ran over, grabbed her, and carried her inside. She's sleeping now, poor kid. Who knows what happened to the rest of her family.

I couldn't believe the news when I turned on the radio this morning. 'War of the Dead' is what they're calling it. I heard one scientist say it had something to do with some groundwater pollutants that have been leaking into the soil for centuries that got activated, they think, by the heat wave. It sounds like anyplace with water treatment plants and industry, all over the country, is at risk or under attack. Well water doesn't sound so backwoods now, huh? It's the chemicals leaching into cemeteries and somehow reanimating corpses in all stages of decay. I don't get it. What the hell kind of chemicals can reanimate a dead body? Maybe that's just the cover story. I know what you're thinking, that I'm way too cynical for a senior. I should lighten up and have more fun. Well, I think cynical may work to my advantage about now.

Prom just isn't going to matter this year, huh? So, according to the news, there has been a lull in zombie related activity when the sun is at its highest point. They think it has something to do with limited eyesight or damaged optical nerves or something from the reanimation process. Dusk and dawn have the highest risk factors.

It figures that some group of science geeks somewhere is already studying and calculating this crap, right?

But after listening to all that, another guy on TV said there was no reason for the dead to walk, and that it could be anything from radiation from space to supernatural reasons.

Huh, who can you believe?

Anyway, I packed up the canned goods and some supplies. I think I'm going to try to make a run for it at noon with Jessica. We're going to head upstate. Local news says that's the safest place right now. Anyplace off the grid is good, in case you get a chance to run, too.

So after draining the lawnmower, leaf blower, and everything else, plus what's in the car already, I got enough gas for about two hundred miles...I think. I sure hope up at your college the dorms are barricaded real tight. Plus, you've got those cinderblock hallways and shit to keep you safe. I hope the electricity keeps working long enough for me to send you word that at least I'm okay when I get where I'm going. Let me know if you're all right, and if you're going to try to relocate at some point.

Maybe we can meet someplace if I live through the night. I'll keep my Blackberry on in case you email me. Good luck, bro.

Ian

```
Date: 11 July 2010 07:57
From: Dan <dtann@gooselabs.com>
To:  Larry <lfey@gooselabs.com
CC: Mark Rivett
Subject: Goose Labs LLC.
```

Hey Larry, I know we've got a ton of work to do today, but I don't think it's a good idea that I come in with everything that's going on.

```
Date: 11 July 2010 8:10
From: Larry <lfey@gooselabs.com>
To: Dan <dtann@gooselabs.com>
CC: Mark Rivett
Subject: Not coming in today
```

Actually Dan, I need you here today. We've had six no-call/no-show's and we have too much work that needs to go out today for you or anyone to be off. I've been trying to call you but something's wrong with your phone.

```
Date: 11 July 2010 08:20
From: Dan <dtann@gooselabs.com>
To:  Larry <lfey@gooselabs.com
CC: Mark Rivett
Subject: Not coming in today
```

I'm sorry, Larry, but it's not safe. There's nothing wrong with my phone, the network's down because of all the stuff going on. There's a news helicopter covering everything live and it's crazy. There's this huge roving mob of those sick people downtown. Police can't get things under control and the hospitals can't handle the injured. I can't believe you're at work. Go home, man! What's more important, some dentist gets his crowns on time or your life?

```
Date: 11 July 2010 08:26
From: Larry <lfey@gooselabs.com>
To: Dan <dtann@gooselabs.com>
CC: Mark Rivett
Subject: Not coming in today
```

Dan, I need you at work now. If you're not here within an hour you're going to be written up. It's perfectly safe. You're not sick. You didn't give any notice for any time off today so you need to be in. I expect you here.

```
Date: 11 July 2010 09:02
From: Dan <dtann@gooselabs.com>
To:  Larry <lfey@gooselabs.com
CC: Mark Rivett
Subject: Not coming in today
```

Ok, Larry, write me up. What's wrong with you? People are dying out there and you expect your employees to risk their lives so you can make your books? A responsible boss would have sent an email telling everyone to STAY HOME!

```
Date: 11 July 2010 09:28
From: Larry <lfey@gooselabs.com>
To: Dan <dtann@gooselabs.com>
CC: Mark Rivett
Subject: Not coming in today
```

Tomorrow we're going to sit down with HR and discuss your insubordination. I'm not sure I need advice on responsibility from YOU on anything, let alone being a boss. But since we're on the subject, a RESPONSIBLE lab tech would KNOW that dentists who don't get their crowns on time become EX clients. I'm at work because that's the responsible thing to do.

```
Date: 11 July 2010 9:35
From: Dan <dtann@gooselabs.com>
To:  Larry <lfey@gooselabs.com
CC: Mark Rivett
Subject: Not coming in today
```

Tomorrow? Are you joking? I'm not leaving my house until this shit is sorted out. Since I already know that sitting down with HR to discuss insubordination means I'm already fired—that's right asshole, I'm still friends with Jenny—who you fired because she wouldn't let you grope her, and Craig, who you fired because you found out he called OSHA on the lab. So I'm just gonna tell you to go fuck yourself.

You're a terrible boss and an even more terrible person! As I write this I am LITERALLY watching a mob of those things moving directly toward the lab. The news helicopter feed is cutting out every couple seconds to edit out people getting RIPPED APART! Do you realize you're probably going to die because you're too stupid to get the hell out of there? That wouldn't be such a bad thing if there weren't a half dozen other tech's you probably bullied into coming to work today who are gonna die, too.

```
Date: 11 July 2010 10:00
From: Dan <dtann@gooselabs.com>
To:  Larry <lfey@gooselabs.com
CC: Mark Rivett
Subject: GET OUT NOW!
```

To everyone at Goose Labs,

Every local news channel that's still running is fixated on a mob of those sick/crazy people roaming around downtown not more than a block away from the lab. Don't risk your life for your job. Get out while you still can!

```
Date: 11 July 2010 10:12
From: Larry <lfey@gooselabs.com>
To: Dan <dtann@gooselabs.com>
CC: Mark Rivett
Subject: Not coming in today
```

Well, if you weren't fired before, you certainly are now. I'll mail you your stuff… whenever I get around to it. It's none of your business why Jenny and Craig got fired so don't go spreading rumors you don't know anything about.

The lab is completely secure but now I'm the only one here thanks to your company-wide email. I'm going to be in contact with my lawyer to pursue action against you to recoup the productivity lost on the day.

```
Date: 11 July 2010 10:27
From: Dan <dtann@gooselabs.com>
To:  Larry <lfey@gooselabs.com
CC: Mark Rivett
Subject: Not coming in today
```

Damn, I will NEVER understand how someone so stupid could ever become anyone's boss. How are you gonna get home? You sleeping in the lab? Did you bring enough food to wait things out? If you bothered to pay attention to anything other than your stupid worthless lab you'd know that they have NO idea when they'll regain control of downtown–could be a week, could be six months. Hope you brought six months of food with you to work today, fucker!

Has it occurred to you that the plate glass door might be secure, but the garage door is open twenty-four hours a day? The goddamn door to the garage doesn't even lock because you're too cheap to buy a new $20 lock! You're dead meat, Larry!

```
Date: 11 July 2010 17:24
From: Dan <dtann@gooselabs.com>
To:  Larry <lfey@gooselabs.com
CC: Mark Rivett
Subject: Ha ha ha ha ha!
```

Hey Larry, just in case you're hiding in the bathroom with your blackberry, I figure it's worth shooting you an email. You're probably hamburger by now, though. Either way, I just saw a big section of that mob break off and disappear into the lab garage on the TV. Good luck, asshole. When all this shit is over, I may not have a job, but at least I'll be alive. That's more than can be said for you, you dumb fuck.

```
Date: 3o July 2010 13:25
From: Harry <HarryHughes@yahoo.co.uk>
To: Meredith <MeredithSmyth-Harding@yahoo.co.uk>
CC: Liam Cadey
Subject: How are you?
```

Dearest Meredith,
I do hope that all is well in France, and that our problems haven't crossed the Channel. What a horrendous situation in which we find ourselves, now that the phones are down; I've had to finally try out this infernal interweb, or whatever you call it.

You were always the technical minded one, with your snazzy new devices and what-nots, but in this case I will admit you were right; it is rather useful!

It's been over a week since we last spoke, but ever the traditionalist, I'm still using my diary, so I have summarized the choicest tidbits for you–and you have no idea how many times this damned computer has infuriated me!

So here goes.

July 21

Well, after we spoke, I took your advice and locked the doors, shuttered the windows and even bolted the back gate! I feel quite safe here, you know. The family house was always designed to keep the riff-raff out—those Georgians really knew how to build a row of houses. Not like nowadays!

My only issue is I'm out of shaving cream, but that is here nor there.

July 22

This was indeed a strange day—Charles arrived, of all people! You remember ever-reliable and over-reliant Charles, don't you? Dressed in his best, as always, but stank to high heaven, even through the door. He must have remembered my address, but I just couldn't face him like that, no matter how much he banged and scratched. Luckily, he went away after a few hours.

July 24

The weather was fine and clear, for a change, so I finally let Dexter out. The poor little chap must have been going stir crazy, having been cooped up with me for the last few weeks!

Other than Charles, I have seen only a few of those 'zombies', as the media likes to call them. Like I've always said, money does buy peace and quiet, and I like to think those living in the area are probably keeping to themselves, just like they did before all this began.

Mind you, I wouldn't like to be down in the city, near those big supermarkets and shopping centers. I've been using father's telescope—you remember the big brass one in the attic?—and the place looks rather hectic; it's positively swarming with the undead things.

July 26

I spent a lot of the day worried, as Dexter didn't come back. You've always said that I needed someone to keep me company, but Dexter has always been company enough. He's not very tolerant of others, as you know!

July 27

Dexter eventually returned, you'll be glad to hear! He was probably gallivanting around dubious neighborhoods, the little bachelor that he is. He was in a grumpy mood though, and clawed me good and proper; I had to lock him in the kitchen.

July 29

I awoke feeling a little flushed, so I decided to pop out for some air. Don't worry, I took one of the pokers from the fireplace, in case one of those blighters came at me. I had become so sick of being inside, I was almost hoping one would!

Old Jamesons' was a mess, which is such a shame really; do you remember when we used to get our weekend sweets there? I didn't see the man himself, but there was a frightful amount of blood by the counter. I do hope the old chap is okay.

I gathered some cat food for Dexter...although when I tried to feed him, he was still terribly off-key. I've left him in the kitchen, I think it's better for the both of us. Maybe he just had enough of me!

You will also be glad to know that I left some money on the counter. Others may stoop to looting, but not I.

July 30
Well, as you know, that's today and I'm dreadfully tired; slept in for the first time in years! I've also lost my appetite, which is most unusual. It must be this damn leg; will have to get some TCP from the shop.
But enough about me, my how I've been rambling!
It's very English of me, but how is the weather in France? It's still cold and damp here, but the view from the attic window is wonderful, and at least the worst of the fires in the city have gone out. There are plenty of Dexter's friends about, too. Maybe they know he's here? But they look a scruffy lot, very little breeding in those scrawny specimens!
Talking of Dexter, I'm sure he's been scratching at the kitchen door since I put him there and I'd be surprised if he hasn't worn a hole in it!
I hope to hear from you soon, Meredith, and do take care of yourself. Make sure that Pierre, or whatever his name is, looks after you! Now, I think I'm going to have a little rest after all this typing.

> Your ever-patient brother,
> Harry

```
Date: 6 July 2010 13:53
From: Mark <Markmiller_22@yahoo.com>
To: Nicky <NICKYstars55@aol.com>
CC: Aaron Rayner
Subject: Farewell
```

Dear Nicky,

The power's finally gone out here so I've had to use my phone line to send this email. I couldn't call you because the lines are too busy, and your mobile's here where you left it. I don't know how long the signal's going to hold up; things have gotten pretty bad. I can still see the lights are on in the distance, so the powers not out where you are, and if you've done what the authorities have been telling everyone, then you've stayed indoors and you're safe. I just hope you're at your computer.

I have to tell you something because I won't get another chance. Firstly, I'm sorry I can't be there to tell you this to your face, but I'm afraid something bad happened earlier. I noticed Mr. Hughes' door was open when I got home; the smell coming from his flat was terrible. I went in to see if he was okay and he attacked me. I managed to get in and lock my door before he could get to me again. He's been there for hours, scratching at the door, only now there's more of them.

They're just like the people from the news, the sick ones, I mean. The moonlight is spilling in through the hallway window, and I can see them clumsily bumping into each other through my spy hole. But even if they weren't out there, I couldn't leave. It's funny, even now with all this going on, it's still hard for me to tell you the truth. The truth is I got scared.

When you first told me I didn't know what to do. I didn't mean to shout at you, and I never meant it when I said it was your fault and that you were trying to trap me. I know now I should have faced up to my responsibilities. I'm sorry. I wish you were here with me now. You don't know how much I want to hold you. How much I want to protect you. The thought of you having to go through it all by yourself breaks my heart. And now with all this going on, it makes it even harder.

I hope you understand why I can't be with you; the last thing I'd want is to harm you or anyone else when it happens. I don't want to die like this, but there's no cure despite what the Government's saying. If there was, then things would never have gotten this bad.

I keep hearing the screams out in the street. I'm too frightened to look outside again. The last time I did, I could see they were everywhere. People were running and trying to get away from them. Most of the houses on the other side of the road are burning and some of the infected people have caught on fire, but they seem totally oblivious to it. All they seem to be interested in is killing and eating us. I don't want to end up like them. That's why I've locked myself in here, then I can't harm anyone. You have to promise me if you get out, that you won't come here and try to find me. It's already too late for me. My whole body's burning with infection and I know I don't have long. I just want you to know I love you and wish I could be there when our baby comes. I never meant for it to end like this. I have to say goodbye now. I think the front door is going to give way; there must be more of them out there now, pressing on it. I need to get to the attic before they do.

Goodbye, my precious Nicky. You were the one thing in my life that made sense. I love you and always will.

Mark

```
Date: 9 July 2010 08:55
From: Mark <MW456@yahoo.com>
To: Bob C <Craft99boss@aol.com>
CC: Jeremiah Coe
Subject: Dear Boss
```

Dear Mr. Craft,

I just wanted to drop a quick line to bring you up to date on the sales call in light of the events sweeping the world.

When Roberts and I landed in Los Angeles, things seemed to still be normal when in fact the dead were already walking. As soon as we stepped foot in the airport, I pulled out my cell phone and tried to call Mr. Patton over at Stand Alone Gaming, to let him know we had arrived and to confirm our appointment for the next day, but I couldn't get through.

Instead, my phone told me, "All circuits are busy."

I tried several more times but got the same result. Roberts tried to call Mr. Patton as well but had the same luck that I did getting through.

Our cab ride to the hotel wasn't all I had hoped for. The DJ on the radio kept talking about riots that had sprung up all over the city, seemingly without any cause. I thought, *Well, this is Los Angeles. If I'm going to be successful in selling advertising out here, I guess I'd better get use to riots,* and put it out of my mind. After all, the riots would have had to have been in the ghetto areas and not in the 90210 district where I'd be staying and working. The talk on the radio didn't bother me, what did was the cabby prattling on incessantly about the violence he had seen that day, strange things like people eating other people, continuing to walk after being shot by police officers and even on fire, without seeming to even realize they were on fire. I remember thinking the man was a nut job and belongs in a locked mental ward somewhere, not driving people around city streets, even the streets of someplace like LA. Now I wish I'd taken his warning and jumped right back on the plane and came home. I patiently listened to the man for the forty-five minute ride while Roberts, the lucky bastard, slept during the entire ride.

Things weren't a whole lot better at the hotel. The first thing we learned from the front desk clerk when we checked in was that they were running severely understaffed and because of this, many of the amenities, like room service, in-room massages and the spa, wouldn't be available until after the riots were over. The clerk said seventy-five percent of their staff had either called in sick or just didn't show up today. If that's the way things work out here, you might want to seriously reconsider opening an LA branch of Craft Advertising. If something as petty as riots are going to stop people from going to work, I'm not sure how viable a business such as yours would be out here.

Roberts and I bummed around the hotel for four hours. We tried several more times to reach Mr. Patton, with both cells and landlines, but we still couldn't get through. With the gym, pool, bar, gift shops and everything else in the place closed, we got bored and caught a cab to a strip club, in an area not having any problems with rioting, of course.

The strip club was every bit as disappointing as the rest of the trip. We got there and sure there were a lot of girls wearing hardly anything, but Roberts and I were two of only a handful of customers in the place. It was dead, sorry for the poor choice of words, but I couldn't think of any other way to describe it. The girls didn't seem interested in dancing and none of the customers in the place seemed to have any interest in watching them dance. Instead, everyone was watching the TVs set up in the four corners of the place. This was where the President announced that the dead were in fact walking. I also listened to some doctor from the Center for Disease Control try to explain in more detail about what was happening, but my head was spinning by then. As you well know, I'm not a fan of the President, but I couldn't imagine even him making that up. At the same time, I couldn't believe it, zombies were things of the movies, not real life.

With nothing going on at the club, we decided to leave. As we were walking out, a man stopped us and asked, "Didn't get what you was lookin' for? I work for a whorehouse, finest bitches in all of LA. I'll take ya if ya want."

Since neither of us is married and neither of us had ever been to a brothel, we decided to go and see what one was like.

Once there, we quickly settled on our girls. I chose a trimmed and toned built brunette and Roberts chose a redhead that could put Dolly Parton to shame in breast size. Roberts chose the sickest looking woman he could and don't take that as a jab towards his taste in women, it isn't, she really looked sick, very sick.

Well, we disappeared into our respective rooms and I don't know what happened, but just as things were heating up with my girl and I, some guy started pounding on the door while yelling, "Get your ass out of this house now!" I recognized the voice as being the manager of the house and did as he said.

Outside, I found Roberts, who looked really pissed. Apparently we got kicked out because Roberts went to the bathroom, and when he came out, his prostitute attacked him. He even showed me the bite mark to prove it.

So we caught another cab back to the hotel and decided to settle in for the night. Things were dull but we passed the time playing Uno. Anyway, Roberts started getting sick. As the hours went by, he kept growing sicker and sicker. Now I know what was happening and what it meant to be bit, but at the time I didn't.

Roberts died, came back, and tried to make dinner out of me. As you know, I wrestled in college, so even reanimated, Roberts didn't have a chance. I grabbed hold of his shirt, rolled to my back, put my feet into his stomach, and kicked off. This had the effect of launching Roberts behind me and through the room's window. He fell nine stories to the ground. I looked out of the window, and even though every bone in his body was broken, I saw Roberts still moving.

Well, Boss, that's pretty much the end of the story. I've kept myself locked up in my room ever since, but I don't know how long I can last here. There isn't any food in the room, and from the sounds of things, the undead now control the hotel so there isn't any way for me to get out of here and find some. As I look out the window, I see power going out all over the city. I think the only reason the hotel still has power is because of its back up generator and I don't know how long that'll last. I figured on the off chance you're still alive and have access to the internet, I'd just let you know what happened to us out here.

Oh, by the way, you know how you told me if I was able to land the Stand Alone Gaming account that you'd make me the head of the LA office of Craft Advertising? Well, after everything I've experienced out here, you can take that job offer and shove it. I QUIT!

Mark Williams

```
Date: 18 July 2010 08:19
From: Jon <Jonathanrivers@live.com>
To: Ben <benmartin@yahoo.com>
CC: Christine Hombrink
Subject: An update for you
```

Dear Benjamin,

I am indeed alive and well, and so are my wife and daughter. In fact, Susan is so well she's taken to ordering Alex around to clean the office, which is where we're holed up. Can't say I'm against the idea of putting her to work, it keeps her mind off of the drama around us. What drama you say? Well besides the whole walking dead situation, we've had a few interesting run-ins with the neighbors.

For example, just yesterday I had to venture out to our car to get Alex's glasses, as she had left them in there the week before this apocalypse hit. We've been searching the internet for escape routes and safe houses, and as you know, Susan and my eyes are about as old as they can get; hard to see the print, you know. Anyway, we needed Alex to read the small bits on the websites so I was sent out to the car to grab her glasses. As I was approaching our BMW—don't even *think* about lecturing me about pretentious cars again, dear friend—Mrs. Cooley ran out from behind the bushes clad only in her raunchy pink feathered bathrobe. I do believe I've mentioned Mrs. Cooley a few times. She's the one who insists on picking up my morning paper and delivering it to me in that disaster she calls a robe. Every morning she slinks across my front lawn and displays herself against my door jam. I've politely told her she needn't bring me my paper— as it's the job of a dog...I didn't add that to my request, I might add—but she insists on doing it. Susan finds it absolutely hilarious and always jokes that Mrs. Cooley is going to steal me away from her one of these days; a blessing in disguise, she tells me.

Back to the BMW...Mrs. Cooley was charging at me, hands raised and drool rippling down her chin, her tongue lolling about. I was armed with Alex's High School Musical umbrella—it has a razor sharp point on the end—and a can of mace. I ducked quickly as she tried to curl her wandering arms around my chest, this time trying to bite me instead of kiss me, and I swung around, hitting her in the back of the head. She stumbled a bit, and I took the chance to run around to the other side of the car. I jumped in and grabbed the glasses from the console. By this time, Mrs. Cooley, in all her sixty-eight years of glory, was spread eagle on my windshield, smashing her head against the glass. I promptly jumped out and gave her a spritz with my mace and a poke with my umbrella, as I dashed like a mad man all the way back inside the sanctuary of my house.

To this hour, Mrs. Cooley is still wandering around my front door, the newspapers at her feet.

On a more serious note, I do hope everything goes well with your wife, Penny. I know what needs to be done, and it's a hard thought to think indeed. But you must remember, that when the change happens, she's not herself. A creature has taken her place, a creature that doesn't share the love, affections, and memories that Penny did. I wish you the best of luck in that endeavor, as I know it's a hard decision to make. Please be safe and careful, whatever you do, and make sure you keep your emotions out of your actions. Penny will eventually be part of the living dead.

You're both in my thoughts.

As for the writing and wine...I have stopped my—infernal, as you put it so gently—writing in order to secure an escape plan for my family, even though I have some amazing ideas for the ending. It's so close to completion! The wine was opened the day the apocalypse hit and the bottle has since been emptied. It was a fine wine indeed, and I will thank you again for such a delightful gift.

Now, on a much more serious note...As far as I can tell, there is an escape route heading up through our state and into Windsor in Canada; Alex has been researching plans since yesterday and this seems to be the best bet for us. I urge you to come with us. I can find a route leading from Virginia to New York and have it emailed to you within an hour's time. I don't want you staying in that house alone, when the time comes, and I don't want you so liquored up you invite the living dead right into your own home!

I do hope you choose to come with us. I can't bear the thought of you going out without me. After all, who am I going to ride with all the way down to Hades' lair?

Please reply back with your decision, Which is yes! In case you were wondering.

Deepest regards,
Jonathan

```
Date: 18 July 2010 12:25
From: Ben <benmartin@yahoo.com>
To: Jon <Jonathanrivers@live.com>
CC: Christine Hombrink
Subject: Got your email
```

Jon,

I'm typing this as fast as my fingers can hobble over the keys, which is not fast at all, you know. I've always been horrible at typing on this stupid contraption, an invention I could do to live without if you ask me...I digress. I'm emailing you an update of what is happening here in Virginia. So far, the outbreak hasn't been contained, but by the sound of what's been playing over the radio, it isn't much different here than it is where you are, in New York.

Penny is still with fever; I have her resting on the couch right now, behind me. The bite mark has grown even more colorful, and has spread over her entire stomach. I fear for her life, but more so I fear for mine, as I know what will become of her after nightfall. I know what I have to do, but dammit, Jon, I don't think I can. She's the love of my life and it pains me to even think about pulling the trigger. The shotgun is loaded and sitting on the bookcase next to this very desk I've claimed for the last two hours. I've been sitting here, wondering about the future, if there is any hope or not for humanity or what has become of it. I have twenty-four hours or so before Penny turns, and between now and then, I plan to fill my glass with enough brandy to satiate all of Russia. That's a lot of brandy, my friend.

I hope all is well with you. Last I heard, you were holed up in the upstairs of your house with your wife and daughter. Are they well? I do hope so. And you're still working on that blasted book? I'm not sure there is even a market for it to speak of now, so I hope you're occupying your mind with ideas of escape and survival. Yes, yes, I know what you're thinking...I never liked the main character of your story anyway, and have sought out any means capable of changing your mind and making that shrew of a man into a hero instead of a villain, but my pleading with you to stop writing and focus on the now has nothing to do with those perfectly valid feelings.

Have you tried the Cabernet I gave you last Christmas? I dare say you had better try it before...well, before anything happens. The year is superb and I spent two week's worth of earnings on that thing. If you passed before you got a taste of it I'd be crushed, and if I ever found out you never opened it, by God we'll meet in Hell and have words, you and I!

Can you tell I'm rambling? In all my years here at the University, I've been telling my English students young and old to stop adding meaningless dribble to their story and just get on with it. But perhaps I see why they keep up their flourish of words, as the nervous thought of completing this email and hitting send will jolt me back to reality, a reality I don't want to be a part of just this moment. Perhaps my students have seen something in a long list of embellished paragraphs and phrases that I haven't...well, haven't until now.

Penny is stirring behind me and I do believe it's time for me to send this email to you. Hopefully it's not the last time that my conscious mind will be able to click this button with this blasted mouse. Please send word with how you and your family are doing, for our correspondence keeps me awake and alert through both anticipation and elation in the findings of your safety. Jon, please don't do anything I wouldn't, or would, for that matter, you know how absolutely mad I am. And please take care of you and yours.
Sincerely,
Benjamin

```
Date: 10 July 2010 07:56
From: Rob <wanderer77@juno.com>
To: Greg <gregsmithh@bellsouth.com>
CC: Rob Rosen
Subject: Resignation
```

Hey Greg,

Unfortunately I won't be in the office today. Or tomorrow. Well, I suppose neither will you, for that matter. See, because you had me work late last night, again, for the third straight night this week, I was outside when the dead invaded the city and began eating everyone. Not you, I suppose, though. You would've been home already. With your wife and kids. Playing Monopoly or Scrabble. Plenty of time to make it down to that nifty basement of yours, behind all that thick steel.

Lucky you, Greg.

Does your shelter have TV, BTW? Could you see the dead walking down your street last night? Could you see them frying to a crisp when the sunlight hit this morning? Now that was a sight to see, let me tell you. In any case, you'll be happy to know, I made it back in time to avoid all that, though I did manage to get bit by some smelly thing that had once been a grandmother. Smelled it, though, and saw it outside my window as everyone on my street was attacked and eaten. Most came back. Still, I'm in one piece, minus the nasty gashes on my neck and thigh, of course.

Anyway, don't worry, I finished the project. On time and under budget, too. Not that there'll be much call for designer sneakers anymore, I'd imagine. Kind of hard for the dead to slip on a new pair of Nikes, Greg. Or take the old ones off. What with our feet being so stiff, and all. Plus, being fashionably barefooted seems kind of the least of our worries, if you see what I'm getting at, Greg.

I mean, besides this intense hunger, mostly for flesh, the human kind, about the only other thing we walking dead have a need for is to keep out of the sun, like I mentioned already. Something to do with our pale and rotting skin, I suppose. Doesn't mix well with sunlight. So much for that vacation of mine in Hawaii, huh? LOL. Besides, tan doesn't really mix well with ashy-gray, does it? Not that you'd know, what with you being home at a reasonable hour, behind all that cold, hard steel. Oh, but I'm repeating myself. Sorry. The old brain is sort of going on the fritz. This is probably the last email I'll be able to manage. Plus, my fingers are about as stiff as my feet now. So much for those designer sport gloves, too, I suppose. Go figure.

Oh, almost forgot the reason for this email. See, I quit, Greg. Not much need for an undead sportswear designer, huh? Then again, I suppose there's not much need for a dead division president either, is there? Can't stay in that steel cellar forever, I mean. Gotta come out sooner or later. Thankfully, last season's track suit makes for a good body cover because I'm headed over there once I hit send, Greg. Kind of got me a taste for some rich food all of a sudden.

Well, that's about it. Hi to the wife and kids, boss. Tell them it'll all be over soon enough. Then we can all play Scrabble together. Big points for six letter words that start with Z and end in E, you know.

So, see you soon, Greg. See you real, real soon.

```
Date: 10 July 2010 11:28
From: Scott <Scottmurry@yahoo.com>
To: Gina <ginacollin@gmail.com>
CC: Scott Cole
Subject: Gonna be late
```

Hey honey,

I just wanted to let you know I won't be home in time for dinner. Ron has me working on this report and he wants it on his desk before I leave—of course. Funny thing is, I don't even know what the hell I'm writing about—for the most part, anyway. You know what I mean.

I just don't get it. Why do I constantly get shit upon by this guy? He's the one who did all the research. Why the hell isn't he doing the writing, too? I mean, seriously...

He researched the markets, and he interviewed all the people involved, but I have to sit here and collect and compile all his notes, his scattered emails, his departmental memos, and his paper scraps and cocktail napkins into some kind of coherent report to show our potential investors. He's probably expecting me to just automatically know half the stuff he never even bothered to write down, too. Ridiculous. Anyway, I don't know why I'm rambling on here. I really need to just dig in and get this thing done. Guess I just needed to rant a bit.

Anyway, the point of all this is...I'm going to be here late tonight. Sorry.

All our phones are down, BTW—which is why I'm emailing instead of calling. This place really is a joke, isn't it? Multimillion dollar deals every other week, but they can't keep the phones up and running for more than three days in a row.

We really ought to switch me over to your cell company, too—I have no signal here. Maybe do a family plan thing or something. I wish this place had windows.

All right, enough, I need to stop procrastinating.

Okay, this is weird. I actually wrote all that like half an hour ago, and was about to send it—then I got pulled away from my desk. Turns out Brian ran to the bank, and got mugged on his way back. I guess a handful of guys just surrounded him, right in front of City Hall, of all places. Looks like he got cut or something. Not really sure what happened—I didn't talk to him, but there was blood all over his arm.

So I guess this is more serious than I thought. They just put the building under lockdown. So it looks like I'm definitely stuck here for a while regardless of what's happening with the report. Apparently, it's some kind of security issue—the guard at the front said something about a gang outside causing trouble.

Oh, and Shelley says she heard Brian say he was bitten, not cut. WTF? Are there roving gangs of hoodlums out there actually biting people now, instead of holding them up with guns? I don't get this city.

Anyway, I should probably wrap this up and send it your way. Don't worry about me, though—we're definitely all safe in here. Although it sounds like Brian and Ron are fighting again... Wow, he's actually growling!

I better go. I'll call you when the phones are back up.

Love you,
Scott

```
Date: 24 July 2010 06:12
From: Neal <STmover@medent.com>
To: Stuart <wendell1@gmail.com>
CC: Marc Shemmans
Subject: Commitment
```

Dear Stuart,

I killed my wife yesterday. I emptied a shotgun into her chest. The glass she was holding looked like it was suspended in the air before it fell to the floor, shattering into pieces.

I haven't been to work for the past month. There's no point after what's happened. I've meditated upon this situation for some time. Even as I type this email, I hear Mary banging around in the cellar, a reminder of the seriousness of this matter.

I take the institution of marriage and bearing of a family very seriously, but this has been tested throughout the developments of the last few weeks.

I don't know if all the madness has spread as far as Australia yet—I've been unable to access TV or radio. For Christ's sake, I don't even know if this email will reach you. But here in the UK, it began July sixteenth. I had taken that day off, planning to spend time with my daughter, Mary, so that my wife, Julia, could be free for the day. Although I can't be sure of the exact time, I believe she left the house somewhere around nine in the morning. The weather was fair, so the children and I spent all morning at the park, navigating the perils of a jungle gym.

By two in the afternoon, I hadn't heard from Julia, and so left a message on her mobile. By five, I had added another three calls and three texts. Julia is a thorough and responsible person who would not normally leave it so long without contacting me.

I don't remember eating dinner that evening. While sitting in front of the television, contemplating the involvement of the authorities, I heard the front door open. The dampness of her clothes and hair wasn't what initially struck me, but rather the blank look on her face. She was bombarded with questions as I wiped her with a towel, but her glassy stare remained frozen. Those eyes didn't look at me, but past me. After stripping off her clothes and conducting a frantic body search, I was able to calm down a bit. There was no sign of obvious trauma, although her skin had been unusually cold to the touch. I guided her to a warm bath where she remained upright, staring straight ahead at the ceramic wall. My volley of questions was met with silence.

I took the rest of the week off. Julia began sleeping increasingly late and refused to eat a bite. The usual exchange of conversation between the children was unnoticed.

By the end of the first week, the blank stares were accompanied by constant drooling. This truly disturbed the children. To break the 'stare' as I called it, I would snap my fingers close to her face, but the blank look remained with a string of saliva growing from her bottom lip.

Walking around the house, I kept a wad of tissues on me, wiping pools of drool off the tables, counter tops and floors. By the second week, Julia looked gaunt. Even when I spoon-fed her, she ate little, the food falling out of her slack mouth.

I telephoned the doctor and asked him to come out to see her, but he told me he was inundated with similar calls and would get to me when he could. I asked him what was wrong with her and he told me he didn't know. He'd never seen anything like it before. I switched on the TV and there they were, walking the city. Hundreds, thousands maybe, all walking around with arms draped by their sides, not exactly swinging, but moving as if they were really no part of them at all. Mouths were hanging open, drooling.

Julia's body odor became unbearable by week three. It wasn't the scent of perspiration or any body fluid, but a rancid smell like rotting meat. Her skin was blue and cold to the touch and a pulse almost nonexistent. Her eyes were a roadmap of crimson vessels and her teeth, the few that remained, were as black as coals.

Despite my constant grooming, I couldn't improve this condition.

One night I awoke to find her gone. I raced down to the kitchen to find her seated there, staring at Mary who was lying dead on the wooden table. I screamed and shouted at her but she just ignored me. Her blank eyes just stared right through me. I tried to physically remove Julia from the house to bring her to the doctor, but she became crazed, a wild animal in suburbia. More than once she tried to bite me. On the second attempt, I saw her front incisor shatter when it narrowly missed the flesh of my wrist. It was after the event that I realized just how dangerous this had become. That night I locked Julia in the attic and buried Mary in the cellar. I did this because I didn't want Julia to be convicted of murder.

The following morning, I entered the cellar and regurgitated the contents of my stomach onto the stone floor. On the concrete floor of the five by seven rooms, was a pile of bones, flesh and gore. As I stepped forward, a whirlwind of flies rose above the mess in a manic fury.

Then something caught my eye. A ring sat atop the mound of corpses. It was Jim's, our next door neighbor's, ring. I had been to the local pub with him enough times to recognize it. He must have come round to check if we were okay and been confronted by Julia.

My wife, the woman I had met in secondary school, made love to by candlelight, taken long walks on the beach and created the life of our beautiful daughter, crawled across the floor, mouth open in anticipation. Her eyes, once blank, now expressed a feeling.

Hunger.

It was then I knew what needed to be done. A theory needed to be tested. I had a gun upstairs, but had never actually fired the weapon. It always sat in my wardrobe, as clean as the day I had bought it. I imagine it had been the assurance of knowing I had the gun that was most important.

I retrieved the gun, and after firing multiple rounds into her, I watched as she remained prone on the floor of the cellar for more than an hour before going upstairs. I tried to keep an objective medical perspective, reminding myself that I hadn't killed my beloved partner. After all, she had stopped breathing the day before.

The next morning, after a brief slumber, I awoke to the sound of scratching at the oak door in the kitchen that led to the cellar. The theory was proven, yet I felt emptier than ever. There she stood at the top of the stairs, sporting several dark holes in her chest. Only this time she stood there with Mary beside her, her small face covered in dirt and blood.

Tears stung my eyes as I gazed at them. I turned and ran into my office upstairs. There I started surfing the web and realized this predicament wasn't confined to just my house. I decided to take a walk and was stunned by what I came across. The streets were deserted, cars were left abandoned, overturned, and burning. There was no one around. Not one person. Only the dead, walking, shuffling, groaning, and eating.

I came home and tried to find out more. I realized there was no radio, no TV. The internet told me there were only a handful of people left in the

UK. I must be one of them. I couldn't find out if it had spread to Europe. I sit here with my laptop in one hand and an axe in the other. I've decided to separate my wife and daughter's head from their shoulders and crush their brains. I do so with regret, but know it will bring them peace and insure the safety of others. I do this out of love for them. I understand the seriousness of this action and the probability that I may not walk away unscathed. That's the price of marriage, to which I'm committed.

Stuart, I hope this email reaches you safely.

Your good friend and brother,

Neal

The Writers

Terry Alexander, Jessica A. Weiss, Dan Larnerd,
Barb Signoretti, Tiara Chukwu, Anthony Giangregorio,
Sean T. Page, David French, Brian J. Smith, Rebecca Besser,
Chris Deal, David Renfrow, Adam Francis Smith, Tony Schaab,
K.M. Rockwood, Liam Cadey, Jeremiah Coe, Kevin Millikin,
Mark Rivett, Rob Rosen, Scott Cole, Marc Shemmans,
Lyle Perez-Tinics, Dane T. Hatchell, Scott M. Baker, Jeff Kelly,
Aaron Rayner, Mike Catalano, Jason D. Brawn, Mariah Deitrick,
Neila Thompson, Michael D. Griffiths, Grady Yandall,
Brianna Stoddard, Tomara Armstrong, Alan Spencer,
Matt Leverton, Domenic Giangregorio, Chelsea Lynn Charters,
Michael Bilinski, E. F. Schraeder, Gary Lucas,
Hollister Ann Grant, Christine Hombrink,
Carrie Cuinn, Tammy Salyer, Kyle Signoretti

PLAYING GOD: A ZOMBIE NOVEL
by Jeffery Dye

It was supposed to be a regeneration virus to help soldiers on the battle-field—regrowing limbs and healing wounds— but a simple act of carelessness unleashed it on an unsuspecting world.

For the virus was not perfected, and once exposed, the host quickly dies, only to rise again as one of the undead.

As countries are quickly overrun, scientists and military teams battle to contain the outbreak.

There is no other option.

If the infection continues to spread, soon the entire globe will be consumed. And perhaps that will be a just punishment for a mankind that dared to try to play God.

DEAD HOUSE: A ZOMBIE GHOST STORY
by Keith Adam Luethke

The old mansion on the edge of town, aptly named Dead House, has a history of blood, pain, and death, but what Victor Leeds knows of this past only scratches the surface of the true horrors within.

But when his girlfriend is attacked by a shadowy figure one rainy night, he soon finds himself caught up in a world where the dead walk and ghostly wraiths abound. And to make matters worse, a pair of serial killers are fulfilling carefully made plans, and when they are done, the small town of Stormville, New York will run red. The last ingredient to open the gates of Hell, and plunge this small upstate town into madness, is rain.

And in Stormville, it pours by the gallons.

The Lazarus Culture
by Pasquale J. Morrone

Secret Service Agent Christopher Kearns had no idea what he was up against. Assigned on a temporary basis to the Center for Disease Control, he only knew that somehow it was connected to the lives of those the agency pro-tected...namely, the President of the United States. If there were possible terrorist activities in the making, he could only guess it was at a red alert basis.

When Kearns meets and befriends Doctor Marlene Peterson of the Breezy Point Medical Center in Maryland, he soon finds that science fiction can indeed become a reality. In a solitary room walked a man with no vital signs: dead. The explanation he received came from Doctor Lee Fret, a man assigned to the case from the CDC. Something was attached to the brain stem. Something alive that was quickly spreading rapidly through Maryland and other states.

Kearns and his ragtag army of agents and medical personnel soon find them-selves in a world of meaningless slaughter and mayhem. The armies of the walking dead were far more than mere zombies. Some began to change into whatever it was they ate. The government had found a way to reanimate the dead by implanting a parasite found on the tongue of the Red Snapper to the human brain. It looked good on paper, but it was a project straight from Hell. The dead now walked, but it wasn't a mystery. It was The Lazarus Culture.

DEAD RAGE

by Anthony Giangregorio
Book 2 in the Rage virus series!

An unknown virus spreads across the globe, turning ordinary people into bloodthirsty, ravenous killers.

Only a small percentage of the population is immune and soon become prey to the infected.

Amongst the infected comes a man, stricken by the virus, yet still retaining his grasp on reality. His need to destroy the *normals* becomes an obsession and he raises an army of killers to seek out and kill all who aren't *changed* like himself. A few survivors gather together on the outskirts of Chicago and find themselves running for their lives as the specter of death looms over all.

The Dead Rage virus will find you, no matter where you hide.

CHRISTMAS IS DEAD: A ZOMBIE ANTHOLOGY

Edited by Anthony Giangregorio

Twas the night before Christmas and all through the house, not a creature was stirring, not even a. . . zombie?

That's right; this anthology explores what would happen at Christmas time if there was a full blown zombie outbreak. Reanimated turkeys, zombie Santas, and demon reindeers that turn people into flesh-eating ghouls are just some of the tales you will find in this merry undead book. So curl up under the Christmas tree with a cup of hot chocolate, and as the fireplace crackles with warmth, get ready to have your heart filled with holiday cheer. But of course, then it will be ripped from your heaving chest and fed upon by blood-thirsty elves with a craving for human flesh! For you see, Christmas is Dead!

And you will never look at the holiday season the same way again.

BLOOD RAGE

(The Prequel to DEAD RAGE)

by Anthony Giangregorio

The madness descended before anyone knew what was happening. Perfectly normal people suddenly became rage-fueled killers, tearing and slicing their way across the city. Within hours, Chicago was a battlefield, the dead strewn in the streets like trash.

Stacy, Chad and a few others are just a few of the immune, unaffected by the virus but not to the violence surrounding them. The *changed* are ravenous, sweeping across Chicago and perhaps the world, destroying any *normals* they come across. Fire, slaughter, and blood rule the land, and the few survivors are now an endangered species.

This is the story of the first days of the Dead Rage virus and the brave souls who struggle to live just one more day.

When the smoke clears, and the *changed* have maimed and killed all who stand in their way, only the strong will remain.

The rest will be left to rot in the sun.

THE BOOK OF CANNIBALS

Edited by Anthony Giangregorio

Human meat . . . the ultimate taboo.

Deep down, in the dark recesses of your mind, can you honestly say you never wondered how it might taste?

Honestly, never wondered if a chunk of thigh tasted like chicken or pork?

Or if a hunk of an arm was similar to steak? And what kind of wine would be served with it, red or white?

Would a human liver be no different than one from a cow, or a pig?

For all we know, human flesh is as tender as veal, better than the finest tenderloin. And that is what the stories in this book are about, eating each other. But be warned, after reading these tales of mastication, you may just become a vegetarian, or at the very least, think twice before taking your first bite of that juicy steak at your local restaurant.

THE TURNING: A STORY OF THE LIVING DEAD

by Kelly M. Hudson

The Dead Walk!

And no place on earth is safe from their ravening hunger. Civilization falls, leaving groups of struggling survivors to navigate a world that has descended into Hell.

Jeff Richards is one such survivor. He and his lover Jenny flee their home in the Bay Area and take a perilous journey through Northern California into Oregon, seeking shelter in rural areas to avoid both the living dead and that most treacherous animal of all: their fellow humans.

But can a man who has lost everything, including his humanity, ever be reborn? When the dead walk, will any of us survive?

Or will we all join the ranks of the undead to forever walk the earth.

VISIONS OF THE DEAD: A ZOMBIE STORY

by Anthony & Joseph Giangregorio

Jake Roberts felt like he was the luckiest man alive.

He had a great family, a beautiful girlfriend, who was soon to be his wife, and a job, that might not have been the best, but it paid the bills.

At least until the dead began to walk.

Now Jake is fighting to survive in a dead world while searching for his lost love, Melissa, knowing she's out there somewhere.

But the past isn't dead, and as he struggles for an uncertain future, the past threatens to consume him. With the present a constant battle between the living and the dead, Jake finds himself slipping in and out of the past, the visions of how it all happened haunting him. But Jake knows Melissa is out there somewhere and he'll find her or die trying.

In a world of the living dead, you can never escape your past.

DEAD MOURNING: A ZOMBIE HORROR STORY
by Anthony Giangregorio

Carl Jenkins was having a run of bad luck. Fresh out of jail, his probation tenuous, he'd lost every job he'd taken since being released. So now was his last chance, only one more job to prevent him from going back to prison. Assigned to work in a funeral home, he accidentally loses a shipment of embalming fluid. With nothing to lose, he substitutes it with a batch of chemicals from a nearby factory.

The results don't go as planned, though. While his screw-up goes unnoticed, his machinations revive the cadavers in the funeral home, unleashing an evil on the world that it has not seen before. Not wanting to become a snack for the rampaging dead, he flees the city, joining up with other survivors. An old, dilapidated zoo becomes their haven, while the dead wait outside the walls, hungry and patient.

But Carl is optimistic, after all, he's still alive, right? Perhaps his luck has changed and help will arrive to save them all?

Unfortunately, unknown to him and the other survivors, a serial killer has fallen into their group, trapped inside the zoo with them.

With the undead army clamoring outside the walls and a murderer within, it'll be a miracle if any of them live to see the next sunrise.

On second thought, maybe Carl would've been better off if he'd just gone back to jail.

ROAD KILL: A ZOMBIE TALE
by Anthony Giangregorio

In the summer of 2008, a rogue comet entered earth's orbit for 72 hours. During this time, a strange amber glow suffused the sky.

But something else happened; something in the comet's tail had an adverse affect on dead tissue and the result was the reanimation of every dead animal carcass on the planet.

A handful of survivors hole up in a diner in the backwoods of New Hampshire while the undead creatures of the night hunt for human prey.

There's a new blue plate special at DJ's Diner and Truck Stop, and it's you!

DEAD THINGS
by Anthony Giangregorio

Beneath the veil of reality we all know as truth, there is another world, one where creatures only seen in nightmares exist.

But what if these creatures do actually exist, and it is us that are only fleeting images, mere visions conjured up by some unknown being.

Werewolves, zombies, vampires, and other lost things that go bump in the night, inhabit the world of imagination and myth, but all will be found in this collection of tales. But in this world, fiction becomes fact, and what lurks in the shadows is real. Beware the next time you sense you are being watched or catch movement in the corner of your eye, for though it may be nothing, it might just be your doom.

THE DARK

by Anthony Giangregorio
DARKNESS FALLS

The darkness came without warning.

First New York, then the rest of United States, and then the world became enveloped in a perpetual night without end.

With no sunlight, eventually the planet will wither and die, bringing on a new Ice Age. But that isn't problem for the human race, for humanity will be dead long before that happens.

There is something in the dark, creatures only seen in nightmares, and they are on the prowl. Evolution has changed and man is no longer the dominant species. When we are children, we're told not to fear the dark, that what we believe to exist in the shadows is false.

Unfortunately, that is no longer true.

SOULEATER

by Anthony Giangregorio

Twenty years ago, Jason Lawson witnessed the brutal death of his father by something only seen in nightmares, something so horrible he'd blocked it from his mind.

Now twenty years later the creature is back, this time for his son.

Jason won't let that happen.

He'll travel to the demon's world, struggling every second to rescue his son from its clutches.

But what he doesn't know is that the portal will only be open for a finite time and if he doesn't return with his son before it closes, then he'll be trapped in the demon's dimension forever.

SEE HOW IT ALL BEGAN IN THE NEW DOUBLE-SIZED 460 PAGE SPECIAL EDITION!

DEADWATER: EXPANDED EDITION

by Anthony Giangregorio

Through a series of tragic mishaps, a small town's water supply is contaminated with a deadly bacterium that transforms the town's population into flesh eating ghouls.

Without warning, Henry Watson finds himself thrown into a living hell where the living dead walk and want nothing more than to feed on the living.

Now Henry's trying to escape the undead town before he becomes the next victim.

With the military on one side, shooting civilians on sight, and a horde of bloodthirsty zombies on the other, Henry must try to battle his way to freedom.

With a small group of survivors, including a beautiful secretary and a wise-cracking janitor to aid him, the ragtag group will do their best to stay alive and escape the city codenamed: **Deadwater**.

DEAD END: A ZOMBIE NOVEL
by Anthony Giangregorio
THE DEAD WALK!

Newspapers everywhere proclaim the dead have returned to feast on the living!

A small group of survivors hole up in a cellar, afraid to brave the masses of animated corpses, but when food runs out, they have no choice but to venture out into a world gone mad.

What they will discover, however, is that the fall of civilization has brought out the worst in their fellow man.

Cannibals, psychotic preachers and rapists are just some of the atrocities they must face.

In a world turned upside down, it is life that has hit a Dead End.

BOOK OF THE DEAD 2: NOT DEAD YET
A ZOMBIE ANTHOLOGY
Edited by Anthony Giangregorio

Out of the ashes of death and decay, comes the second volume filled with the walking dead.

In this tomb, there are only slow, shambling monstrosities that were once human.

No one knows why the dead walk; only that they do, and that they are hungry for human flesh.

But these aren't your neighbors, your co-workers, or your family.
Now they are the living dead, and they will tear your throat out at a moment's notice.

So be warned as you delve into the pages of this book; the dead will find you, no matter where you hide.

ANOTHER EXCITING ADVENTURE IN THE DEADWATER SERIES!
DEAD SALVATION
BOOK 9
by Anthony Giangregorio
HANGMAN'S NOOSE!

After one of the group is hurt, the need for transportation is solved by a roving cannie convoy. Attacking the camp, the companions save a man who invites them back to his home.

Cement City it's called and at first the group is welcomed with thanks for saving one of their own. But when a bar fight goes wrong, the companions find themselves awaiting the hangman's noose.

Their only salvation is a suicide mission into a raider camp to save captured townspeople.

Though the odds are long, it's a chance, and Henry knows in the land of the walking dead, sometimes a chance is all you can hope for.

In the world of the dead, life is a struggle, where the only victor is death.

INSIDE THE PERIMETER: SCAVENGERS OF THE DEAD
by Alan Spencer

In the middle of nowhere, the vestiges of an abandoned town are surrounded by inescapably high concrete barriers, permitting no trespass or escape. The town is dormant of human life, but rampant with the living dead, who choose not to eat flesh, but to instead continue their survival by cruder means.

Boyd Broman, a detective arrested and falsely imprisoned, has been transferred into the secret town. He is given an ultimatum: recapture Hayden Grubaugh, the cannibal serial killer, who has been banished to the town, in exchange for his freedom.

During Boyd's search, he discovers why the psychotic cannibal must really be captured and the sinister secrets the dead town holds.

With no chance of escape, Broman finds himself trapped among the ravenous, violent dead.

With the cannibal feeding on the animated cadavers and the undead searching for Boyd, he must fulfill his end of the deal before the rotting corpses turn him into an unwilling organ donor.

But Boyd wasn't told that no one gets out alive, that the town is a death sentence. For there is no escape from *Inside the Perimeter*.

DEADFALL

by Anthony Giangregorio

It's Halloween in the small suburban town of Wakefield, Mass.

While parents take their children trick or treating and others throw costume parties, a swarm of meteorites enter the earth's atmosphere and crash to earth.

Inside are small parasitic worms, no larger than maggots.

The worms quickly infect the corpses at a local cemetery and so begins the rise of the undead.

The walking dead soon get the upper hand, with no one believing the truth. That the dead now walk.

Will a small group of survivors live through the zombie apocalypse?

Or will they, too, succumb to the Deadfall.

LOVE IS DEAD: A ZOMBIE ANTHOLOGY
Edited by Anthony Giangregorio
THE DEATH OF LOVE

Valentine's Day is a day when young love is fulfilled.

Where hopeful young men bring candy and flowers to their sweethearts, in hopes of a kiss...or perhaps more. But not in this anthology.

For you see, LOVE IS DEAD, and in this tome, the dead walk, wanting to feed on those same hearts that once pumped in chests, bursting with love.

So toss aside that heart-shaped box of candy and throw away those red roses, you won't need them any longer. Instead, strap on a handgun, or pick up a shotgun and defend yourself from the ravenous undead.

Because in a world where the dead walk, even love isn't safe.

UNITED STATES OF ARMAGEDDON
by Jeffrey Thomas Crooms
THE END OF A COUNTRY!

America's enemies plot a sadistic plan to destroy the population and armed forces so they can swoop in and rule the country.

Terrorists called the Horsemen smuggle in a deadly biological weapon straight to the heart of the United States and release it.
The result is a land covered with corpses, bloated bodies strewn from sea to sea.

A few desperate survivors battle through the blighted landscape on a last ditch mission to save the country from total domination.

But the biological weapon has a side effect, one no one would have ever foreseen, one too unimaginable to even contemplate.

Welcome to the future. Welcome to the Unite States of *Armageddon*

BOOK OF THE DEAD
A ZOMBIE ANTHOLOGY VOL 1
ISBN 978-1-935458-25-8
Edited by Anthony Giangregorio

This is the most faithful, truest zombie anthology ever written, and we invite you along for the ride. Every single story in this book is filled with slack-jawed, eyes glazed, slow moving, shambling zombies set in a world where the dead have risen and only want to eat the flesh of the living. In these pages, the rules are sacrosanct. There is no deviation from what a zombie should be or how they came about. The Dead Walk.

There is no reason, though rumors and suppositions fill the radio and television stations. But the only thing that is fact is that the walking dead are here and they will not go away. So prepare yourself for the ultimate homage to the master of zombie legend. And remember... Aim for the head!

REVOLUTION OF THE DEAD
by Anthony Giangregorio
THE DEAD SHALL RISE AGAIN!

Five years ago, a deadly plague wiped out 97% of the world's population, America suffering tragically. Bodies were everywhere, far too many to bury or burn. But then, through a miracle of medical science, a way is found to reanimate the dead.

With the manpower of the United States depleted, and the remaining survivors not wanting to give up their internet and fast food restaurants, the undead are conscripted as slave labor.

Now they cut the grass, pick up the trash, and walk the dogs of the surviving humans.

But whether alive or dead, no race wants to be controlled, and sooner or later the dead will fight back, wanting the freedom they enjoyed in life.

The revolution has begun!

And when it's over, the dead will rule the land, and the remaining humans will become the slaves...or worse.

KINGDOM OF THE DEAD
by Anthony Giangregorio
THE DEAD HAVE RISEN!

In the dead city of Pittsburgh, two small enclaves struggle to survive, eking out an existence of hand to mouth.

But instead of working together, both groups battle for the last remaining fuel and supplies of a city filled with the living dead.

Six months after the initial outbreak, a lone helicopter arrives bearing two more survivors and a newborn baby. One enclave welcomes them, while the other schemes to steal their helicopter and escape the decaying city.

With no police, fire, or social services existing, the two will battle for dominance in the steel city of the walking dead. But when the dust settles, the question is: will the remaining humans be the winners, or the losers?

When the dead walk, the line between Heaven and Hell is so twisted and bent there is no line at all.

RISE OF THE DEAD
by Anthony Giangregorio
DEATH IS ONLY THE BEGINNING!

In less than forty-eight hours, more than half the globe was infected.
In another forty-eight, the rest would be enveloped.
The reason?
A science experiment gone horribly wrong which enabled the dead to walk, their flesh rotting on their bones even as they seek human prey.

Jeremy was an ordinary nineteen year old slacker. He partied too much and had done poorly in high school. After a night of drinking and drugs, he awoke to find the world a very different place from the one he'd left the night before.

The dead were walking and feeding on the living, and as Jeremy stepped out into a world gone mad, the dead spotting him alone and unarmed in the middle of the street, he had to wonder if he would live long enough to see his twentieth birthday.

THE CHRONICLES OF JACK PRIMUS
BOOK ONE
by Michael D. Griffiths

Beneath the world of normalcy we all live in lies another world, one where supernatural beings exist.

These creatures of the night hunt us; want to feed on our very souls, though only a few know of their existence.

One such man is Jack Primus, who accidentally pierces the veil between this world and the next. With no other choice if he wants to live, he finds himself on the run, hunted by beings called the Xemmoni, an ancient race that sees humans as nothing but cattle. They want his soul, to feed on his very essence, and they will kill all who stand in their way. But if they thought Jack would just lie down and accept his fate, they were sorely mistaken. He didn't ask for this battle, but he knew he would fight them with everything at his disposal, for to lose is a fate worse than death.

He would win this war, and he would take down anyone who got in his way.

THE WAR AGAINST THEM: A ZOMBIE NOVEL
by Jose Alfredo Vazquez

Mankind wasn't prepared for the onslaught.

An ancient organism is reanimating the dead bodies of its victims, creating worldwide chaos and panic as the disease spreads to every corner of the globe. As governments struggle to contain the disease, courageous individuals across the planet learn what it truly means to make choices as they struggle to survive.

Geopolitics meet technology in a race to save mankind from the worst threat it has ever faced. Doctors, military and soldiers from all walks of life battle to find a cure. For the dead walk, and if not stopped, they will wipe out all life on Earth. Humanity is fighting a war they cannot win, for who can overcome Death itself? Man versus the walking dead with the winner ruling the planet. Welcome to *The War Against Them*.

DEADTOWN: A DEADWATER STORY
B OOK 8
by Anthony Giangregorio

The world is a very different place now. The dead walk the land and humans hide in small towns with walls of stone and debris for protection, constantly keeping the living dead at bay.

Social law is gone and right and wrong is defined by the size of your gun.
UNWELCOME VISITORS

Henry Watson and his band of warrior survivalists become guests in a fortified town in Michigan. But when the kidnapping of one of the companions goes bad and men die, the group finds themselves on the wrong side of the law, and a town out for blood.

Trapped in a hotel, surrounded on all sides, it will be up to Henry to save the day with a gamble that may not only take his life, but that of his friends as well.

In a dead world, when justice is not enough, there is always vengeance.

END OF DAYS: AN APOCALYPTIC ANTHOLOGY
VOLUMES 1-4
Edited by Anthony Giangregorio

Our world is a fragile place.

Meteors, famine, floods, nuclear war, solar flares, and hundreds of other calamities can plunge our small blue planet into turmoil in an instant.

What would you do if tomorrow the sun went super nova or the world was swallowed by water, submerging the world into the cold darkness of the ocean? This anthology explores some of those scenarios and plunges you into total annihilation.

But remember, it's only a book, and tomorrow will come as it always does. Or will it?

Twisted Fish
An Aquatic Anthology
Sturgeon's lotion
PlayFish
Edited by
Anthony Giangregorio

THE BOOK OF CANNIBALS

ISBN 13: 978-1-935458-52-4   ISBN 10: 1-935458-52-3

ARE YOU HUNGRY YET?

THE PLACE TO GO FOR ZOMBIE AND APOCALYPTIC FICTION

LIVING DEAD PRESS

WHERE THE DEAD WALK

www.livingdeadpress.com

Blood of the Dead
A.P. Fuchs

Bits of the Dead
edited by
Keith Gouveia

Axiom-man
The Dead Land
A.P. Fuchs

Wicked East Press
Publisher of Fine Fiction Anthologies

coming soon...

www.wickedeastpress.com

www.ingramcontent.com/pod-product-compliance
Lightning Source LLC
Chambersburg PA
CBHW070951180726
48291CB00004B/1246